To Dad
Fathers Day
1996

Paul & Lynda

This Ruth

HAROLD S. PAISLEY

ALSO BY HAROLD S. PAISLEY

The Gospel of Mark
The Believer's Hymn Book Companion
This Daniel

This Ruth

This Ruth
Harold S. Paisley

OlivePress
2333 Main Street
Glastonbury, CT 06033
800.832.7081

Copyright © 1995 by OlivePress

FIRST EDITION
ISBN 0-9631200-2-6

This Ruth

HAROLD S. PAISLEY

Dedication

This Ruth is dedicated to my wife, Rosetta, who encouraged me in the writing of this devotional study on the book of Ruth; to our daughter, Ruth, and the many Ruths who have supported me in various ways during 50 years in the Lord's work.

Contents

Preface

It has been with joy and pleasure that I have carefully read over each word of this devotional commentary. It is honoring to the Lord Jesus, the great Redeemer. Boaz was "a mighty man of wealth" and his cost in redeeming the lost inheritance of Elimelech was very great, but the cost was not so very great that it cost him all he had. He did not become poor. Our blessed Redeemer "was cut off and had nothing." "When He found one pearl of great price, He went and sold all He had and bought it." His grace was so great that "for your sakes, He became poor." The comparisons and the contrasts between Boaz and Christ are vividly described by Harold Paisley.

All of this and very much more is the substance of this beautiful commentary. It will stimulate the mind of the reader, but it will also reach the heart. May the response of every heart fulfill the meaning of the name of Obed (a worshipping servant)!

We owe a great debt of thanks to our beloved brother and friend for this Christ-exalting work on the Book of Ruth.

N. Crawford

Foreword

Naomi looked away. The footprints a husband and his family had left on the road from Bethlehem to Moab had settled back to dust; yet, the sorrow and scars of the journey were forever etched in her heart. On the road she traced Orpah's footprints growing smaller and fainter in the distance. Naomi glanced at the feet planted so firmly before her own. She listened as Ruth lifted up her eyes and through her tears whispered, "Thy God shall be my God." And so a new journey began.

It is a privilege to publish Mr. Paisley's ministry on the book of Ruth. *THIS RUTH* details the remarkable experiences of Ruth the Moabitess. The portrait of the life of Ruth is warm and touching. Against a background of sorrow and heartbreak, a story of love, hope and blessing unfolds in all its richness.

Mr. Paisley skillfully examines the characters moving through the book of Ruth. While the paths may seem to weave and wander, he guides us with careful exposition and traces God's guidance and leading each step of the way.

THIS RUTH presents God's tremendous plan of redemption and the blessings to follow. Mr. Paisley writes, *The Holy Spirit, who inspired its writing, had in view a wonderful unfolding of divine links in the glorious subject of redemption, presenting in typology our Lord Jesus Christ as the Kinsman-Redeemer.*

Mr. Paisley reminds our hearts of the One who walked without shoes— face stained with spittle— through the gate, outside the city. He tenderly bids us stand beside the cross to view the Blessed Redeemer— bruised, beaten, and nailed to the tree. In the dark hours at Calvary, the Redeemer lifted up His eyes and, through the blood and tears, whispered, "My God, my God, why hast thou abandoned me?" Forever, the Redeemer will bear the marks of the journey in His blessed hands, feet and side.

THIS RUTH thrills the soul. Stoop in the field beneath the midday sun, hear the gentle promise of Boaz in the early hours, and see the child cradled tenderly in Naomi's arms.

It is my earnest prayer that *THIS RUTH* will warm the heart and bring blessing to all its readers.

Paul Tornaquindici

Introduction

The title "This Ruth" is based on the question of Boaz, "Whose damsel is this?" Ruth is the name of one of the most delightful books in the Old Testament. Remarkable for its brevity, its eighty-five verses are easily read in twenty minutes. Precious for its deep unfolding of the Person of Christ, the mysteries of redemption, and the future of Israel, the charming and beautifully written story is both simple and sublime — a gem of literature and a veritable wonder of language.

The great Benjamin Franklin, though not a professing Christian, recognized the literary excellence of the book of Ruth. It is recorded that when representing the newborn republic of America at the French capital, he was indignant when he heard learned and polished men ridiculing the Bible and expressing surprise that any one should ever spend time reading it.

Franklin one day announced to them that he had a copy of a very ancient manuscript, and invited them to his apartments on a certain evening to hear it read. At the time appointed, his literary friends were all present and he had an accomplished elocutionist read to them his copy of the manuscript. They were loud in their praise of it, and the most critical of them pronounced it to be superior to anything they had ever read or listened to, and asked if they might have copies. Imagine their astonishment when the ingenious American informed them, with a twinkle in his eye, that they had been listening to one of the sixty-six books of that collection called the Bible for which they had affected such contempt. It was the book of Ruth, with the name of God omitted, and a few other slight alterations made by Franklin, so that the infidel Frenchmen might not suspect it was the Bible that was being read to them.

There is great value in the historical information contained in Ruth. Life is described in a provincial town in Israel in the days of the judges. Aspects of kinship, marriage, local customs and the institution of redemption form the background to the book. The responsibility of the go'el (kinsman-redeemer) is illustrated more fully in the book of Ruth than anywhere in scripture. Here we have a key to a knowledge of the go'el. He was the redeemer. If one had to sell property, the go'el could buy it to protect the elimination of a family heritage. This book also gives an example of the law of liverate marriage recorded in Deuteronomy, chapter twenty-five, verses five to ten. A widow without a child should be taken by her next of kin to wife, so that the firstborn which she bore would succeed in the name of the dead husband, that his name would not be blotted out of Israel. The law of liverate is so called from "liver" which means brother-in-law. If any brother-in-law failed to act as a kinsman-redeemer in a case of this kind, the woman could bring him to the elders of the land. If he still refused to perform the action of a go'el, then the widow should loose his shoe from his foot and spit in his face. His name shall be called in Israel: The house of him that hath his shoe loosed. In this delightful book the go'el performed fully the kinsman's part by redeeming the property and taking the widow as his bride.

vi

Another beautiful feature of the book is the record of the compassionate provision of God for Gentiles. This fact is also one of the leading themes of another little book of four chapters — Jonah. The story of Ruth unfolds the wonder of God's generous love for the homeless, lonely and hungry. Ruth, without a husband, without a home, without adequate food, found a kinsman-redeemer — a man named Boaz who provided her with bread enough and to spare and a home in his house at Bethlehem to share his love. In this the story speaks to all who were strangers afar off, lonely, homeless, and starving until we were found of the Redeemer.

Ruth is rich in dispensational, doctrinal, devotional and didactic pictures. Its interest touches aged and youthful, rich and poor, master and servant, husband and wife, widow and fatherless, believer and unbeliever. One can learn the value of the little books of the Bible which often yield bread to the eater, seed to the sower and a full basket for the worshipper.

It is interesting to note that only two books in the Old Testament have as their title the name of a woman. One was a Gentile (Ruth) and the other a Jew (Esther). Ruth became the bride of the wealthy kinsman-redeemer, a man who feared God. Esther became the queen of one of the world's greatest empires and was the wife of the heathen monarch. Both became a source of great blessing to the world. God has distinguished them by placing their names at the head of two inspired books of the Bible. Thousands of baby girls have been named after both Ruth and Esther. The holy influence of Ruth has endured centuries of time, and has been known around the world.

In the marriage of these two women, God has given two great tokens that Gentiles were to be blessed only through Abraham's seed (Genesis 12:3, 22:18; Psalm 72:17; Acts 3:25).

The book of Ruth has been described as a cameo of love and a key to the doctrine of redemption.

Apart from its literary excellence, historical importance, typical import, prophetic pictures and doctrinal shadows, the story of Ruth is rich in moral and spiritual lessons. The faithful yet gracious ways of God are evident with spiritual dealings with souls. His judgment in government, grace in restoration, sovereignty in purpose, provision in redemption and glory in kinship, are pictured in the book. The Holy Spirit reveals to those who meditate upon Ruth, wondrous things from this delightful part of the Word of God.

If there is one lesson above another in the spiritual life that the book of Ruth teaches, it is the emphasis placed upon the results of placing full confidence and trust in God. When life's greatest choice came to Ruth, she abandoned all past interests, choosing God as her God, and His people as her people. From that time of trust and confession, on the Bethlehem road, she went on steadily and humbly in the path of devotion and faith. The results of her leaving Moab's idolatry neither she nor Boaz lived to see, but we know, for out of their union there came the continuation of the line of the Messiah.

"Remember that of the work you do today you cannot see the issue. It is wrought through faith in God. It may be in some great city, or a hidden village among the hills, that your life may be lived, small, unknown, never published, yet you may be God's foothold for things to come, which if told you now you would not possibly believe." (Campbell Morgan)

The "Gleanings" in this field of scripture is with one vital end in view, that with the writer, each reader may be more devoted to Christ, in order that, by our loyalty, He may win the victories of His Royalty.

Harold S. Paisley

Overview

Before considering each of the four beautiful chapters of this delightful portion of God's Word, an overview of its fascinating arrangement would increase our appreciation of the many facets of precious truth revealed in what otherwise would be looked upon as a simple, pastoral idyll. The Holy Spirit, who inspired its writing, had in view a wonderful unfolding of divine links in the glorious subject of redemption, presenting in typology our Lord Jesus Christ as the Kinsman-Redeemer. The vital and all important Messianic line, from which the Saviour came, is the climax of the book (chapter 4:18-22).

THE AUTHOR AND DATE

The author of the book is unknown, but since the genealogy terminates at David, it would seem evident that it was written by an inspired writer during the time of David's reign. To place it later, to a period after the exile, is incorrect. Any reader can plainly see at once its place in the days when the judges ruled. Some ascribe its authorship to Samuel. In all probability this Jewish tradition may be correct. The date of writing seems to be around 1011 - 97 B.C. before Solomon's reign, or the writer would have included his name in the genealogy. The book would be of great interest to David as Ruth was his great-grandmother. How he would thank God for His grace! The book was also a delight to Solomon, for one of the pillars set up at the entrance to the temple which he built, was called Boaz. He could thank God for divine strength in his honored ancestor, whose name means "in him is strength."

THE TITLE

The book is named Ruth. Like the Book of Esther, Ruth is one of the smaller historical books of scripture. They are the only two books in the Old Testament bearing the names of women. Ruth was a Gentile and Esther a Jewess. Both honored the Lord above all others in their time by showing great devotion and determination to be faithful to God in difficult circumstances. Both were finally honored by God.

Five books are called "The Megilloth" by the Jews and are read by them at festive celebrations commemorating great historical events in their past history: The Song of Solomon at Passover; Lamentations on the ninth day of the month AB in memory of the destruction of Jerusalem; Ecclesiastes at Tabernacles; Esther is read when they celebrate Purim (Esther 9:28), and Ruth is the special book read at Pentecost.

There is only one reference to Ruth in the New Testament, but this reference shows the great importance of her biography preserved in the Old Testament, as it appears in the royal genealogy of the Lord Jesus (Matthew 1:1-5). In the fuller genealogies of 1 Chronicles 1 her name is not found. Her name appears twelve times in the book which, chosen by God, has her name as title, giving her an honored mention in the Old Testament. In the solitary mention in the New

Testament (Matthew 1:5), God has placed her alongside divinely honored men as Abraham, David and Solomon. But sovereign grace has linked the Moabitess stranger not only with David the king, but with Jesus the Messiah, the King of Glory. These facts should stir our hearts to place a very special interest in the study of the book that is titled "Ruth."

THE SETTING

This is most important and may be considered in two ways: I. Time Setting and II. Literary Setting.

As to the first: When did it happen? The last verse of Judges (21:25) states "In those days there was no king in Israel. Every man did that which was right in his own eyes." This is contained in the first verse of Ruth, "Now it came to pass in the days when the judges ruled." Again the last verses of the book show that it connects the history in Judges with that in 1 Samuel. It forms an appendix to Judges and an introduction to Samuel. It is not in chronological order, however, but is likely set early in the Book of Judges. What a choice outline of the possibility of living a life of piety and purity in the midst of idolatry and rebellion! Ruth presents true devotion in the midst of days of departure. How refreshing to turn from the distress of Judges to the peace of Ruth!

As to the placing of Ruth in the literature of the Bible, it could have been written into Judges. The design of arrangement shows divine handiwork. It is a rare gem in its setting. Its place between these two books of Judges and Samuel enhances its beauty.

What is the outstanding spiritual lesson of the Book of Judges? A statement repeated often in the early chapters indicates the cause of the shameful declension of Israel in Canaan after the death of Joshua. *And the children of Israel did evil in the sight of the Lord (chapter 3:7,12; chapter 4:1, chapter 6:1, etc.).* In chastisement, God al-

3

lowed enemies to oppress them, but when they cried to Him in their distress, He raised up judges who delivered them. Yet, after each deliverance, the people forgot the Lord and lapsed into evil. They were led away into the wicked ways of the heathen. They failed to honor the living and true God and continued in a path of evil in His sight. Who was behind the evil? We are sure it was the power of the evil one, Satan himself. In our day, the same evil power is at work to hinder spiritual progress (Ephesians 6:11,12).

What is the outstanding spiritual teaching in 1 Samuel? If in Judges the power of Satan is evident, in 1 Samuel the power of the flesh is seen. The early chapters speak of three couples: two women, two men and two kings: Peninnah and Hannah (chapter 1), Eli and Samuel (chapter 3), Saul and David (chapter 16). In each of these the principle of the flesh in opposition to that which is spiritual is recorded. In the Book of Ruth the influence of the world as typified in the land of Moab completes the picture of the threefold hindrance to all spiritual testimony. The wonderful progress seen in Ruth's experience, in the midst of the dark picture of Israel's apostasy, the workings of the flesh and the seductions of the world, present bright gleams of God's grace. In the midst of national disorder, individual departure, and spiritual decline — God was working for the accomplishment of His promise of that seed of Abraham, who would bring blessings to all nations. Hence, while the Book of Ruth begins with the flight of Elimelech from Immanuel's land, it closes with the name of David, of whom the Lord said, *I have found David, the son of Jesse, a man after mine own heart, which shall fulfill all my will, ...of this man's seed hath God according to His promise brought unto Israel a Saviour, Jesus (Acts 13:22,23).* This is a complete summation of the purpose of Ruth, preparing the way, not for David alone, but for his greater Son.

Undoubtedly, this little book of personal history well deserves the separate and distinct place given it in the canon of Holy Scripture. Mr. William Kelly has written in his interesting "Lectures On The Earlier Historical Books," "But while there can, to my mind, be no reasonable question that Ruth follows Judges, it is equally plain, that it appropriately forms a book to itself, and is a natural and necessary preface to the first Book of Samuel."

THE SCENES

The period of time covered in the book is around 20 years. There are four outstanding scenes, which form a normal outline to the beautiful story.

1. Moab (chapter 1:1-18). Period about 10 years.
2. Bethlehem - field of Boaz (chapter 2:19, 2:23). Some months.
3. Bethlehem - Threshing floor (chapter 3). One night.
4. Bethlehem - The city (chapter 4). One year.

The first great scene is on the highway where Ruth expressed her outstanding devotion. Her wonderful words are precious — there is nothing like them anywhere in literature (Ruth 1:16,17).

The second scene is in the field of Boaz near Bethlehem, where Ruth displayed her continued diligence (Ruth 2:7).

The third scene is in the threshing floor at Bethlehem, where Ruth made her greatest request (Ruth 3:9).

The fourth scene is in the city gate at Bethlehem, where Ruth received her glorious reward (Ruth 4:9-11).

It is interesting to note that the first three chapters deal with the personal life of Ruth; she expressed her personal choice and she personally elected to work in the field. She made request at the feet of Boaz through personal desire.

These illustrate the personal matters between believers and the Redeemer. However, in the last chapter, her destiny and links with the redeemer are in public display. There her choice and service are climaxed by his reward and love being shown to all. One day it will be true of all His people — what we have chosen, where we have labored — all that we have been — will be openly owned by our Blessed Lord Himself.

THE STORY

The contents are perfectly simple and easy to understand from a straightforward reading of the book, which can easily be completed in twenty minutes. Briefly it tells of the leaving of a family of four, who turned away from Bethlehem-judah in a time of famine and sojourned in the land of Moab. This was a wrong pathway. The two sons married Moabite women, following the death of their father. Later, the sons died and Naomi and her two daughters-in-law were left widows in Moab. In her sad plight, news reached Naomi of the Lord's visitation with bread in Bethlehem, so she decided to return. Ruth and Orpah started the journey with her. Orpah finally went back to Moab and her gods, but Ruth accompanied Naomi all the way to Bethlehem. The story goes on to tell of Boaz, the rich kinsman, who not only treated the widows kindly, but eventually married Ruth the Moabitess, and redeemed the inheritance. The book ends with a brief but important genealogy in which the name of Boaz is prominent as the great-grandfather of David, through whom would come the Messiah, Christ the Lord. In this ending is the main purpose of the book, to trace the line of descent of the Messiah, who was to be of the tribe of Judah (Genesis 49:10) and is here revealed as coming from the family of David (2 Samuel 7:12-16).

THE SPIRITUAL TEACHING

The key word is go'el. It appears at least eleven times. This word go'el, kinsman-redeemer, gives a beautiful view of the Lord Jesus as such in the Gospel by Luke and the Epistle to the Hebrews. There

6

were two important laws given in Israel, one referring to the redemption of an inheritance, and the other to the redemption of a person (Leviticus 25, Deuteronomy 25). In the case of an inheritance being sold, or of a person, the redemption must be made by one near of kin. He must therefore have the right by birth, he must have the means, and he must have the willing heart to do the work. A responsibility also rested upon the redeemer to marry the widow, so as to raise up a progeny to the dead husband. He also must buy the inheritance. The two great points for the go'el were union and purchase. The promised results were redemption, rest, love, fruit and blessing.

How fully this is typified in Isaiah where, in that great prophetical book, Christ is presented as the Go'el of Israel. The keyword of Isaiah is Redemption. Twenty-four times we read of the Redeemer, the redeemed or redemption.

THE SIGNIFICANCE OF NAMES

Names mean little to us: We use them simply for identification of persons. It is otherwise with Bible names. Parents expressed their godly desires for their children by given names at birth. In this faith and hope was made known. Many examples support this idea, e.g. Elimelech "Elohim is King," Elisha "salvation is on Elohim," Elijah "Jehovah is God." However, some parents changed the name later because of disappointment in early traits of character. Some names were also changed for one more noble as Abram "exalted father," who became Abraham "father of a multitude" (Genesis 17:5). It is evident that the parents of Nabal, whose name means "fool," renamed him in keeping with his ways, for none would give such a name at birth. Abigail, Nabal's wife, who was a woman of good understanding, stated of him *as his name is, so is he: Nabal is his name, and folly is with him (1 Samuel 25:25). Even a child maketh himself known (obtaineth a name) by his doings, whether his work be pure, and whether it be right (Proverbs 20:11).* This indicates the difference in names given by aspiration and names by character.

In the Book of Ruth the naming of Elimelech and Naomi was an indication of the hopes of God-fearing parents, while in the naming of Mahlon and Chilion we have an example of the earliest manifestations of their physical health, and their parents' loss of hope.

Each of the seven personalities in Ruth is introduced by an interesting expression, "and the name of the man (or woman) was...." The literal name has a spiritual significance, indicating a clue to the divine teaching in the happenings in the history of each of the seven persons mentioned. The meanings of their names, as given in the Newberry Bible are very valuable and informative:

Elimelech	"my God is King"
Naomi	"my pleasant one"
Mara	"bitter"
Mahlon	"sick"
Chilion	"pining"
Orpah	"neck, hind or fawn"
Ruth	"beauty" or "friendship"
Boaz	"in him is strength"

It is of interest to draw attention to the Septuagint where the Book of Ruth is entitled "Routh," the Greek equivalent of the Hebrew name. This name may be interpreted "friendship."

It is also shown in the Newberry Bible the names by which God reveals Himself in this Book of Ruth. These names reflect various revelations of His ways and purposes. In one name or another the reader is enabled to catch glimpses of His ineffable glory. The many names given to God in His Word contain unfoldings of His person, attributes, character and interests. This great subject of the names of

God is largely unknown even to Christians. There are sixteen names in the Old Testament, to be distinguished from many descriptive titles. Most precious is the final name revealed by His Son: "Father," essentially a New Testament revelation.In the Book of Ruth, God is made known as:

Elohim (chapter 1:16) "The Triune God"
Jehovah (chapter 1:8) "He that is, and that was, and that is to come"
El Shaddai (chapter 1:21) "The Almighty. All Sufficient"
Jehovah the Lord (chapter 1:21) "The Everlasting One"
Jehovah Elohim (chapter 2:12) "The Lord God"

To trace the use of these various names in the context by Naomi, Ruth and Boaz, reveals the manifold goodness of God. What His grace plans, His power perfects. He is indeed Elohim, Jehovah, El Shaddai.

THE STUDY OF THE BOOK

Various methods of study are available. We suggest five:

I. DEVOTIONAL

One outstanding lesson for spiritual development is the example of the fruitful results of purpose of heart in seeking the will of God and His pathway for our lives. When life's great choice came to Ruth, she decided aright, and from that day onward her steadfast path of faith and trust is an outstanding pattern for young believers. The words of Solomon, her great-grandson, are an epitome of her life, *The path of the just is as the shining light, that shineth more and more unto the perfect day (Proverbs 4:18).*

II. DISPENSATIONAL

The dispensational application of the story of Ruth is full of interest, outlining in typical illustration the purpose of God in connection with Israel. Ruth is usually given as a type of the church, as the bride of Christ. The use of such an idea is of value as a picture, but primarily the beauty of the type to Israel has many blessed lessons.

Naomi represents the nation as a whole, presently in unbelief and bitterness. In Elimelech and his two sons we see the complete breakdown of testimony for God, once entrusted to His chosen people. Naomi, setting her steps homeward once more, indicates the return of Israel to their land. Others are affected as is suggested in the concern of Orpah and Ruth to return with Naomi. Two parts of Israel are indicated, one with worldly aspirations going back to the idolatry of Moab, the other a picture of the godly remnant searching for the blessing of knowing the God of Israel, cleaving to the promises of the Word of God. Of these we quote the writer to the Hebrews, *We are not of them who draw back onto perdition, but of them that believe unto the saving of the soul (Hebrews 10:39)*, an apt description of Orpah and Ruth. The remnant returning with the nation to the homeland will finally be linked with the mighty Kinsman-Redeemer and inherit all the blessings of His reign. In this application some have found difficulty in the fact of the Gentile origin of Ruth. How can she represent the godly remnant? God speaks of the present state of Israel on par with the condition of Gentiles. They are "Lo-ammi", which description means "not my people" (Hosea 1:9). The wondrous grace which called Gentiles out of darkness, which in the past were not a people, but are now the people of God (1 Peter 2:9,10), will also call, draw and save a remnant Israel *according to the election of divine grace (Romans 11:5,6)*. Many scriptures will enlighten the student of these great truths of Israel's future restoration, and the faithful remnant's devotion to the Redeemer. Such chapters as Hosea 2,3,5,6, Isaiah 53, 54, 55, Jeremiah 31, 32, 33, Romans 9, 10, 11, will open up the important teaching of Israel's future of earthly and spiritual blessing through the Redeemer — our Lord Jesus Christ and their Messiah.

III. TYPICAL

Most of the teachings in this realm center around the seven personalities in the book, whose significant names have been already indicated. Elimelech, Mahlon, and Chilion are types of backsliders from God, whose restoration is not evidenced. Naomi, in contrast, is a backslidden saint who is happily restored to the Lord. In her restoration, blessing is brought to others and abundant fruitfulness for generations to come. Ruth is a type of a sinner, who through links with believers, trusted the Lord. The evidence of her prior faith was openly confessed in one of the greatest statements in the Bible. William Bryan expressed the thoughts of many hearts when he wrote of the noble confession of Ruth: "We cannot hope to contribute to literature a sentence so exquisite and so thrilling as that into which Ruth poured the full measure of a noble heart, but we can imitate her in devotion — the brightest jewel in her crown." The heart of Ruth was fixed. She was steadfast in faith. Orpah is a sad type of those who show some interest in spiritual things, but turn back and perish, a solemn picture of apostasy (Hebrews 6:4-6).

Boaz is a beautiful type of the Lord Jesus as the redeemer and strength of his people: *Their Redeemer is strong. The Lord of Hosts is His name. He shall thoroughly plead their cause that He may give rest (Jeremiah 50:34).* These words of Jeremiah, given by the Lord, point back about 600 years to Boaz as a picture of the coming Redeemer who would be born 600 years after his prophecy.

IV. ANALYTICAL

Chapter One: This chapter begins with a famine and ends with a harvest. God's dealings are presented in three distinct ways, in keeping with His names: Jehovah (verse 8), Elohim (verse 16), El Shaddai (verse 21). I. **The God of Government** (1:1-5); II. **The God of Recovery** (1:6-18); III. **The God of Grace** (1:19-22).

Chapter Two: This chapter enlarges on the "provision" envisaged in chapter 1:22. The two needy widows arrived in Bethlehem at the very time when the barley harvest was ready for reaping. Three important subjects are the main themes of chapter two: I. **The Presentation of the Redeemer** (2:1-4); II. **The Prosperity of the Field** (2:5-16); III. **The Progress of the Stranger** (2:17-23).

Chapter Three: A spiritual mind is required to apply the precious truth of this holy chapter. In contrast to the field where with others Ruth shared fellowship and food and the ministry of the redeemer, we are now introduced to her private communion with Boaz. Three sections may be observed: I. **The Present Ministry of the Redeemer** (3:1-2); II. **The Preparation Suitable for the Presence of the Redeemer** (3:3-7); III. **The Promised Prospect of the Redemption** (3:8-18).

Chapter Four: Of this chapter it can be said *Better is the end of a thing than the beginning* (*Ecclesiastes* 7:8). Ruth begins with burial but ends with birth, begins with famine and ends with fame. In the first three chapters, Ruth is prominent, but in this chapter Boaz is preeminent. Again there are three parts: I. **The Supremacy of the Redeemer** (4:1-12); II. **The Satisfaction of the Widow** (4:13-17); III. **The Selection of the Royal Line** (4:18-22).

V. EVANGELICAL

Some splendid gospel messages can be based on incidents in this beautiful book. We give one example: In the field of Boaz, the type of Christ the Saviour and Redeemer, Ruth appeared as a stranger who knew him not, yet he knew her and all concerning her past. So with the sinner and Christ. Ruth took her true place in his presence as a stranger not deserving anything. This is a fine illustration of how God meets those who own their need (1 Timothy 1:15). Boaz commanded his servants to present handfuls of purpose to the seeking one. These picture the great gospel texts telling of God's love, provision and offer (John 3:16, 5:24, Acts 16:31, etc.). Grace brings the gospel like "handfuls of purpose" within easy reach, but the sinner must receive them and then beat them out, which speaks of appropriating the great salvation personally.

The Purposes
of God

The first chapter of Ruth contains some of the greatest language in literature: the confession of the filial love and unswerving piety of Ruth the Moabitess. There are three great movements which may be considered as follows: I. **The actions of God in government** (verses 1-5); II. **The dealings of God in goodness** (verses 6-18); III. **The purposes of God in grace** (verses 19-22).

I. THE GOD OF GOVERNMENT: EL SHADDAI

One of the interesting features of the scriptures is flexibility of application. In our study of this delightful book we would endeavor to comment on each section in its historical context and prophetical indications, and finally apply the happenings recorded practically. In so doing we desire that unfoldings of the beauties of the Redeemer, His name and work, may bring exaltation to His name and gladness to many hearts. No other book contains such universal appeal. Met together in its eighty-five verses are young and aged, poor and rich, servant and master, obedient and disobedient, believer and unbeliever.

We have indicated that the opening verses of chapter one disclose God working in government. The words of Naomi on her return to Bethlehem seem to indicate the dealings of God in her experience, "El Shaddai hath dealt bitterly with me." It seems the suited name of God for this first section.

The first mention of this distinctive name, found forty-eight times in the Old Testament, occurs in Genesis 17:1. When Abram had passed through a long testing time, all hope that he should have a son promised by God was so long deferred that his self-sufficiency was at an end. In this time of crisis, God appeared to him and said, "I am El Shaddai." We adhere to the traditional view that Shaddai is derived from the word used often in the Word of God for the breast of a mother. Dr. Campbell Morgan stated, "The name El Shaddai is peculiarly suggestive, meaning literally: the Mighty One of Sufficiency." As Abram heard for the first time that name spoken in a human ear, how he must have been comforted. The new understanding of the Almighty One as indicated in the word El, is joined by the gracious word Shaddai, which goes further and reveals tender compassion and perfect supply.

It is also an arresting fact that, out of the forty-eight mentions of this wondrous name, thirty-one are found in the Book of Job. In no other part of God's Word is the tender love of El Shaddai more evident than to the one who was so oppressed. Job held to his knowledge of this God and was able to rise higher than any other in his outstanding declaration of faith. *Though He slay me, yet will I trust in Him (Job 13:15).*

Naomi joins with Abram and Job in her use of His gracious name, when she returned to Bethlehem. Those who recalled her asked "Is this Naomi?" She replied "Call me not Naomi (pleasantness). But call me Mara (bitterness), seeing the Lord hath testified against me and El Shaddai hath afflicted me." The name of the One who had spoken in government is also the One who will prove Himself to be the God of sufficiency. Every child of God who knows Him as El Shaddai will find comfort in times of testing, when He may seem afar off; in the end we will bless the hand that guided. For what His goodness plans, His power perfects. He is still God Almighty, El Shaddai.

Now it came to pass in the days when the Judges ruled that there was a famine in the land. And a certain man of Bethlehem-judah went to sojourn in the country of Moab, he, and his wife, and his two sons. (1:1)

The first and last verses of the Book of Ruth show its link with the history in Judges and 1 Samuel, forming an appendix to the one, and an introduction to the other. The happenings in Ruth took place in the days when judges judged. The history of those days in the Book of Judges present a long succession of dark scenes of departure from God. These resulted in unhappy oppressions of Israel, bloodshed and violence, discord among the tribes, and famines in the Land of Promise. The days were marked by lawlessness. *Every man did that which was right in his own eyes (Judges 17:6, 21:25)*. In such conditions of confusion, ungodliness, immorality and apostasy, we turn with delight to consider alongside such dark events, the bright gleams of God's gracious mercy disclosed in the Book of Ruth. In the very midst of disorder and unrest is this beautiful description of a peaceful, God-fearing community in complete separation from the evil times and actions of the world of those days. It is an ancient example showing how it is possible to live and share with others, piety, purity, and prosperity in the midst of lawlessness, anarchy, and sin.

It would be difficult to state the exact historical setting of the story of Ruth in the Book of Judges. However, most agree it was in the early part of Judges. Boaz being son of Rahab, who appeared at the time of the conquest of Jericho, which was around forty years before the judges, would indicate that events recorded in the Book of Ruth transpired early in the days of Israel's settlement in Canaan.

There was no king in Israel in those days, which was the root cause of the serious disorder (Judges 21:25). They had forsaken God as their King, disowning His authority. However, there was a faithful remnant who owned Jehovah's Name in a scene so confused the God of Government moved unseen for the accomplishment of His promise through the seed of Abraham, who would bring blessing to all the nations of the earth (Genesis 22:15-18, Galatians 3:16).

Accordingly, God sent a famine, resulting in a family of four leaving Immanuel's land and the fields of Bethlehem for an enemy land and the fields of Moab, thereby forming the great link in the chain of Messianic history. Hence the book ends with the name of David of whom God could say, *A man after mine own heart* —a description found in the Book of Acts 13:22.

It may be that the famine is the one in the days of Gideon (Judges 6:34). This famine was a mark of God's governmental dealings because of His displeasure on account of their departure from His ways. The Land of Promise was 'a land that floweth with milk and honey" indicating milk from well-fed herds, and honey from abundant vegetation. The Lord, by the word given to Moses, described in beautiful language the prosperity of the land. Before they entered their inheritance, however, the annual harvests would be dependent on their love and obedience to Jehovah.

Take heed to yourselves that your heart be not deceived, and ye turn aside and serve other gods...and Jehovah's wrath kindle against thee, and he shut up the heavens that there be no rain, and that the ground yield not its produce, and ye perish from off the good land which the Lord giveth you (Deuteronomy 11:16,17). From this scripture we can plainly learn that in the land of Canaan famine was a means of chastisement used by God for the correction of His people. His government of them in departure was to reveal His goodness in their recovery. The brief statement, "There was a famine in the land" states the fact, but the earlier scriptures (Deuteronomy 11:1-17) show the cause.

On account of the famine a certain man of Bethlehem-judah went to sojourn in the country of Moab: he, his wife and his two sons. To this man, the obvious course was to emigrate to another more fruitful place, and thus escape starvation for himself and his family. This man of Bethlehem had not considered the sad effects upon the life and testimony of the father of the nation. He followed in the same path as Abram, failing to observe that the example had a sad sequence. Abram was faced with a famine in Canaan and to evade it went down into Egypt. He learned that God would not permit him to make his home in Egypt. In his dealings as the God of Government He plagued Pharaoh to bring Abram out of Egypt (Genesis 12:10-20).

There were two men in Bethlehem-judah who faced the same famine. What a difference in their actions. Boaz passed through the testing time of famine. Trusting God, he proved God. Elimelech failed in the test and went to sojourn in Moab, which became for him the end of testimony—a place of death.

It is worthy of remark that Bethlehem has a special place in scripture. Because of the varied references to it, we are more familiar with the name than any other place mentioned in the early scriptures. In the Book of Ruth, Bethlehem, the place of restoration and joy, is in direct contrast with Bethlehem, the place of apostasy and sorrow in the histories at the end of the Book of Judges (chapters 17:7; 19:1,2).

Bethlehem is a village five miles southwest of Jerusalem, 2550 ft. above sea level, in the hill country of Judea, on the main highway to Hebron and the land of Egypt. In Jacob's time it was called Ephrah, which means "fruitful." In the conquest of Canaan it was called Bethlehem-judah (Ruth 1:1) to distinguish it from the town of Bethlehem (Joshua 19:15) in Jebulun, now the village of Beit Lahm, seven miles northwest of Nazareth.

The first mention of Bethlehem is on the occasion of the birth of Benjamin (son of my right hand) called by Jacob, while Rachel, his mother, called him Benoni (son of my sorrow, Genesis 35:18,19). In the Book of Ruth, Bethlehem is associated with Boaz, the kinsman-redeemer. Here also David kept his father's sheep and was anointed king by Samuel (1 Samuel 16:12-15). Hence it was known as the City of David (Luke 2:4).

Micah, in his great Messianic prophecy (Micah 5:2), used a different name calling it "Bethlehem-Ephratah." Though it was little among the thousands of Judah, He would come forth who would be the Shepherd Ruler of Israel (Micah 5:1,2). *"Whose goings forth have been from of old, from the days of eternity"* (*Newberry*). Bethlehem is kept before the reader of the Old Testament—until at last the Heavenly Host hail there the hour in which the Son of God became the Son of Man (Luke 2:11).

Benjamin's sonship and sorrow, Boaz's kinship and redemption, David's shepherding and kingship, all combine to typify the One who is altogether lovely, our Lord Jesus Himself.

In the time of the famine in the land, a man belonging to this place withdrew. His wife, under the influence of her husband, was forced to join him. She was manifestly a woman of singular piety and strength of character. The two sons also were influenced by their father's departure.

The man went to sojourn in the country of Moab. This statement shows his backslidden condition. Departure from the inheritance was a complete breakdown in faithfulness to God. *So shall not the children of Israel remove from tribe to tribe, for everyone of the children of Israel shall keep himself to the inheritance of the tribe of his fa-*

thers (*Numbers 36:7*). He intended to sojourn for awhile until conditions improved in his homeland, but for him and his two sons it was for their remaining lifetime.

The lessons of this first verse apply to saints in all ages and contain three great principles for our learning: 1. The principle of lawlessness; 2. The principle of backsliding; 3. The principle of influence. In the first we learn that the events to follow took place *in the days when there was no king in Israel: every man did that which was right in his own eyes* (*Judges 21:25*). In the second, we see an example of the proverb, *The backslider in heart shall be filled with his own way* (*Proverbs 14:14*). In the third concerning influence, the words of Romans 14:7, *None of us liveth to himself,* all of us are an influence for good or evil.

And the name of the man was Elimelech, and the name of his wife Naomi, and the name of his two sons Mahlon and Chilion, Ephrathites of Bethlehem-judah. And they came into the country of Moab, and continued there. (1:2)

This verse introduces the names of the family who emigrated from Bethlehem (the house of bread), to the more fruitful country of Moab. These four names have great significance, and are not mentioned elsewhere in the scriptures. Often in the Old Testament histories, names afford a key to the moral and scriptural instruction contained in the passages where they occur. In this book the meaning of the names clearly emphasizes the spiritual teaching of the history. It is interesting that the seven names of the narrative are given to no other persons in the scriptures together; Elimelech, Naomi, Mahlon, Chilion, Ruth, Orpah, and Boaz are exclusive and significant.

Elimelech means "My God is King." No other has this name. The meaning contrasts with the condition of the times in which

Elimelech lived—"In those days there was no king in Israel." This man had a name which should have been a testimony to the nation that God was their King. He was placed by God; a silent witness of the royal tribe of Judah, to the sovereignty of Jehovah over His redeemed. Alas, in the distress of famine, he left his place of service and went to Moab to dwell among a people whose origination was abominable (Genesis 19:35-38).

God also introduces Naomi, Elimelech's wife, and his two sons in the same language. *The name of his wife Naomi, and the name of his two sons Mahlon and Chilion.* Naomi's name is unique to the Bible, and appears to mean "pleasantness." It expresses the spiritual grace and beauty of her womanhood. The proverb of Solomon could form a fitting description, *Her ways are ways of pleasantness, and happy is everyone that retaineth her (Proverbs 3:17,18).* However, the influence of her husband led her into a way which resulted in sadness, but happily in the end she found again that all her paths were peace.

The names of Mahlon and Chilion are also full of meaning, the usual being "sickness" and "pining." The deterioration from the high qualities indicated in the parental names is evident. The thought of descension from the spirituality of the former generation is indicated. This feature is one of the marks of our age also.

They are described as Ephrathites of Bethlehem-judah. The abundant productivity of the vicinity around Bethlehem, with its fruitful fields, vineyards and olive groves, was indicated in its names. Ephrata, which means fruitfulness, was an ancient name of the region around Bethlehem, which means "house of bread." Micah in his delightful prophesy states that out of "Bethlehem Ephratah," while little among the thousands of Judah, the Shepherd Sovereign would come (Micah 5:1,2). Ephrath was Bethlehem's name when Rachel, the mother of Benjamin, died, whose names "son of my sorrow" and "son of my right hand" pointed onward to the suffering

Son to be born in Bethlehem, who would finally be the Sovereign Son to reign from shore to shore (Genesis 35:16-19).

With such a background of blessing from God at Bethlehem, one is surprised that Elimelech could leave the place where God's honor dwelt to go to sojourn in a place of vile idol worship. Backsliding is to be feared. To dwell in fellowship with God in days of famine will always bring final delight. *Trust in the Lord and do good, so shalt thou dwell in the land, and verily thou shalt be fed (Psalm 37:3).*

Moab represents, in its origin, moral impurity (Genesis 19:35-38) and in its history, spiritual enmity against God's chosen people (Numbers 22:1 and Joshua 24:9,10). Egypt in scripture sets before us the world of art, learning, and pleasure, marked by absolute independence of God and His authority. How sad to read of Abraham going to Egypt. The Sodom world is marked by features so evident today, of a debased society, of immorality and lust. Toward this Sodom world Lot pitched his tent. Babylon points to the religious world which denies the great fundamentals of the faith once for all delivered to the saints (Jude 3). This form of the world is defiling. Daniel was carried to it but purposed he would not be defiled by it. The warning for believers today is *Come out from among them and be ye separate (2 Corinthians 6:14-18).* There are further indictments against Moab. *Moab hath been at ease from his youth up, and hath settled on his lees, and hath not been emptied from vessel to vessel, neither hath he gone into captivity: Therefore his taste remained in him, and his scent is not changed (Jeremiah 48:11).*

To such a place Elimelech, taking his family, went to sojourn for a while, intending to return when the famine ended. However, he became a settler, and ended his life, as did his two sons, in that heathen land. The present day lesson is obvious. Many, to evade conditions which arise among God's people as a result of departure from His Word, leave the place and location of testimony to visit in what appear to be more fruitful fields. They intend to be visitors but soon become settlers, and are never recovered, often dying away from the fellowship of those who own the Lordship of Christ and the authority of His Word.

And Elimelech, Naomi's husband died: and she was left, and her two sons. And they took them wives of the women of Moab; the name of one was Orpah, and the name of the other Ruth: and they dwelled there about ten years. And Mahlon and Chilion died also both of them: and the woman was left of her two sons and her husband. (1:3-5)

Elimelech, the head of his family, had led them astray. He was acquainted with the history and doings of Balaam who induced the people of God to join themselves to Baal-Peor, and to indulge in the idolatry of the gods of Moab. He knew also of the thousands who perished from the plague that followed. This was one of the darkest pages in Israel's history. It is an event mentioned for the warning of God's people even in our day (1 Corinthians 10:8 and Revelation 2:14).

Because of the conduct and character of the Moabites, God had said, *Thou shalt not seek their peace nor their prosperity all thy days forever* (Deuteronomy 23:4-6 and *Nehemiah* 13:1,2). In spite of the plain warnings of God in His word, Elimelech went amongst these people to seek bread. Finally, God, in His governmental dealings, cut him off. The house of the emigrants from Bethlehem became a house of mourning. The sons, soon after the death of their father, took to themselves wives of the women of Moab. Mahlon took Ruth and Chilion took Orpah. An Israelite might not marry a Canaanitish woman (Deuteronomy 7:3) and a Moabite might not be received in the congregation of Jehovah (Deuteronomy 23:3), but the marriage of an Israelite with a Moabitish proselyte woman was not prohibited.

A careful reading of Deuteronomy 23:3 states that a Moabite, masculine, shall not enter into the congregation of the Lord. Therefore Ruth was not excluded. In the Book of Ruth she is designated "Ruth the Moabitess" five times (Ruth 1:22, 2:2, 21 and 4:5,10). Marriages with seven different nationalities were forbidden by God (Deuteronomy 7:1-4) lest they would turn away Israel's sons from following the Lord. Why no prohibition from marriage with a Moabitess? While some teach that Boaz by grace set aside God's law and Ruth was received into the congregation as an exception, such cannot be proven from God's Word. Matthew, in his wonderful genealogy of Jesus Christ, the Son of David, the Son of Abraham, supplies the answer in the inclusion of Ruth in the royal line of Judah (Matthew 1:1-6). God had made divine provision that the Moabitess taken into that line from whence Messiah was to be born, would by His will be a suitable instrument of continuing the succession of the royal line of Judah whereby His Son would be brought into the world.

Of this we can only say, *O the depth of the riches both of the wisdom and knowledge of God! How unsearchable are His judgments and His ways past finding out! For who hath known the mind of the Lord? Or who hath been his Counselor? For of Him, and through Him, and to Him are all things: to Him be glory forever (Romans 11:33-36).*

Ten years passed and with sudden brevity the record states, *Mahlon and Chilion died also, both of them, and the woman was left of her two sons and her husband (Ruth 1:5).* Here is described the triple sorrow of Naomi: Three graves in a strange country. Pleasantness becomes bitterness. Within one household are three widows bearing burdens of loneliness, tears and anxiety. The question of Naomi's heart would be "Doth Jehovah care?" Yes, she was the object of His concern, and soon she would know His love which has no limit and grace without measure. The beautiful words of Annie Johnston Flint seem appropriate. One of the great secrets of the hymns and poems of Miss Flint was that she wrote from her heart as a result of the experiences of her life, the greater part of which was spent in pain endured with great patience. At twenty years of age, so crippled with arthritis she was unable to walk, she wrote some of her most beautiful and touching poems, including the fragrant lines of "He Giveth More Grace"

He giveth more grace when the burdens grow greater
He sendeth more strength when the labors increase
To added affliction He addeth His mercy
To multiplied trials, His multiplied peace.

When we have exhausted our store of endurance
When strength has declined ere the day is half done
When we reach the end of our hoarded resources
Our Father's full giving is only begun.

His love has no limit, His grace has no measure
His power no boundary known unto men,
For out of His infinite riches in Jesus,
He giveth, and giveth, and giveth again.

How applicable are these words to all the Lord's people, who like Naomi, are plunged into bereavement and sorrow!

II. THE GOD OF GOODNESS: ELOHIM

In the study of the scripture there can only be one interpretation of a portion, but it may have many applications. Now, while it is most important to be clear about interpretation, both in one's own mind and when speaking, yet it is the application of the Word which enhances the value and beauty of the Bible. The adaptability of the

Book is one of its great charms, providing food for the soul and instruction for the spirit, from that which otherwise might seem profitless. For instance, think of the events in the pathway of the Lord which are fraught with moral lessons to us, and also with prophetical foreshadowings. Consider His parables and their manifold significance. How broad is the view, how vast the design, and how many-sided are the aspects of the divine truth! They make a spiritual mosaic, which the spirit of truth alone can put together, the forms and colors of which unite and blend in one harmonious whole. This gives added interest to the beauty of the Book of Ruth.

Paul, when writing of happenings in the history of God's people on their journey from Egypt to Canaan, stated, *Now these things were our examples....Now all these things happened unto them for examples, and they are written for our admonition upon whom the end of the ages are come* (1 Corinthians 10:6-11). Again Paul wrote, *For whatsoever things were written aforetime were written for our learning, that we through patience and comfort of the scriptures might have hope (Romans 15:4).*

With this in view, a study of the lives and characters of the various individuals in the Book of Ruth teaches lessons for believers of all ages. The problems and perplexities of Naomi, Ruth and Boaz provide examples of lives through which God was pleased to reveal patterns for godliness. Those who place all their confidence in Him will be tenderly carried as Israel of old, of whom the Lord said, *I bore you on eagles wings and brought you unto Myself (Exodus 19:4).* This part of chapter one (verses 6-18) has two distinct parts: I. **Commencing the journey** (verses 6-7); II. **Choosing at the crossroad** (verses 8-18).

COMMENCING THE JOURNEY

Then she arose with her daughters-in-law, that she might return

from the country of Moab: for she had heard in the country of Moab how that the Lord had visited His people in giving them bread. Wherefore she went forth out of the place where she was, and her two daughters-in-law with her, and they went on the way to return unto the land of Judah. (1:6,7)

Some touching things concerning Naomi should be considered in these verses, *The woman was left* (verse 5). What a melancholy state, alone, being in a country of strangers. She had accompanied her husband and her sons, having no other option, into the land of Moab. To all appearances Naomi was desolate. There is nothing in the human heart dreads so much as the thought of being utterly alone. Everyone longs to have a human hand in theirs in the great crises and troubles of life. There is One, the Friend that sticketh closer than a brother, who has promised that He will never leave us nor forsake us, even when we faint by the way and fail Him in our fidelity. Although Naomi was in a country of idolatry where false gods as Chemosh (Numbers 21:29) were worshipped, she had a vital interest in the land of Judah. Evidently there were lines of communication kept open by her with the Lord's people in the land of Judah, which was home to her (verse 21). Naomi had also been a clear witness for God in Moab. Her first recorded words reveal that she was a woman of prayer (verses 8-9). Would she not recall that God executeth the judgment (guardianship) of the widow and loveth the stranger (Deuteronomy 10:18)?

Naomi's sons had married Moabitesses and had died childless. Many mothers-in-law and daughters-in-law are not on good terms. However, Naomi enjoyed love and kindness from her two daughters-in-law all the years she had known them in Moab. Now, as she prepared to return to Bethlehem, they joined her as she went forth to commence the pathway to the land of Judah. If in Elimelech's history there is the path of backsliding and God's governmental deal-

30

ings—in Naomi we see the path of restoration and God's goodness. What moved her to return? Was it the sorrow of loneliness and loss? No! It was the good news from the far country that created a thirst in her soul to go forth from the place where she was. *As cold water to a thirsty soul, so is good news from a far country* (Proverbs 25:25). Earlier in the scriptures "good news" that Joseph was alive and lord of all Egypt caused Jacob to say, *I will go and see him before I die* (Genesis 45:26-28). The prodigal was moved to leave the misery and hunger of the far country when he recalled bread enough and to spare in his father's house. The goodness of God led to his repentance. His words seem to echo the experience of Naomi, *I will arise and go to my father* (Luke 15:18). Naomi in the land of Moab had known what it was to have the Lord taking away from her, but now tidings reach her ears of God in goodness again giving bread in Judah. The expression "The Lord visited His people in giving them bread" has a close connection with the language of Luke 7:16, "God hath visited His people." The reader's mind is thus drawn onward from the history of Boaz and Ruth at Bethlehem to that of the Lord Jesus Christ, who was the true Bread who came in grace to Bethlehem.

The commencement of Naomi's journey homeward had an effect upon her two daughters-in-law so that they went "with her." The piety of Naomi had power over their hearts. She illustrates the words written hundreds of years later, *If any obey not the word, they also may without the word be won by the conversation of the wives* (1 Peter 3:1). It appears that, by her conduct of a meek and quiet spirit, her testimony to the God of Israel bore fruit in a place of sinful idolatry. The silent preaching of one woman in a foreign land was used to win the love of one like Ruth, whose open confession of Elohim revealed the truth of her conversion. How great a lesson for all believers to be missionary in character, for *He that winneth souls is wise* (Proverbs 11:30).

CHOOSING AT THE CROSSROAD

And Naomi said unto her daughters-in-law, Go, return each to her mother's house. The Lord deal kindly with you, as ye have dealt with the dead, and with me. The Lord grant you that ye may find rest, each of you in the house of her husband. Then she kissed them, and they lifted up their voice and wept. And they said unto her, Surely we will return with thee unto thy people. And Naomi said, Turn again, my daughters. Why will ye go with me? Are there yet any more sons in my womb, that they may be your husbands? Turn again, my daughters, go your way: for I am too old to have a husband. If I should say I have hope, if I should have a husband also tonight, and should bear sons, would ye tarry for them till they were grown? Would ye stay for them from having husbands? Nay, my daughters. For it grieveth me much for your sakes, that the hand of the Lord is gone out of me. And they lifted up their voice and wept again. And Orpah kissed her mother-in-law, but Ruth clave unto her. And she said, 'Behold thy sister-in-law is gone back unto her people, and unto her gods. Return thou after thy sister-in-law. And Ruth said, Intreat me not to leave thee or to return from following after thee: for whither thou goest, I will go; and where thou lodgest, I will lodge; thy people shall be my people, and thy God my God; where thou diest, will I die, and there will I be buried: The Lord do so to me, and more also, if ought but death part thee from me. When she saw that she was steadfastly minded to go with her, then she left speaking unto her. (1:8-18)

This most interesting section is worthy of prolonged meditation. The scene on the highway: The three widows had walked quite a distance. In all possibility they had reached the ford of the river Arnon, on the northern boundary of Moab. There Naomi called a halt. The daughters-in-law realized they had not fully counted the cost of continuing all the way to the land of Judah. They have now reached the crossroads, not only on the road, but in spiritual choice. It was to witness the parting of the way for Orpah and the complete consecration of Ruth to continue her walk with the Lord, for the rest of her life. As we view the remarkable occasion on the Bethlehem road, how profound are the lessons.

The words that close the tenth chapter of Hebrews seem to illuminate the widows and their thoughts (Hebrews 10:32-39).

1. Naomi on the road of restoration: *But call to remembrance the former days in which after ye were illuminated...cast not away therefore your confidence, which hath great recompense of reward. For ye have need of patience, that after ye have done the will of God, ye might receive the promise (Hebrews 10:32-36).*

2. Orpah on the road of renunciation: *If any draw back, My soul shall have no pleasure in him (Hebrews 10:38).*

3. Ruth on the road of resolution: *But we are not of them who draw back unto perdition (as Orpah): But of them that believe to the salvation of the soul (Hebrews 10:39).*

The scene on the Bethlehem road opens with the three widows conferring together. They may be regarded as typical characters. There is Naomi, picture of a backslider, who had left the good land, for the enemy's country. She whose name "Naomi" means "pleasant" had become "Mara" — "bitterness." Orpah, the worldling, had come part of the way but returned to her own land and its evil worship of Chemosh — the god of stone. In contrast there was Ruth, the simple and determined believer whose choice and subsequent course we are to follow. In these we learn that the backslider's path is ever bitter, the worldling is satisfied with the world, but the believer with the Lord. It is the story of the apostasy of a sinner, the recovery of a saint and the consecration of a young believer. This section introduces us to the main form of diction used by the Holy Spirit in the divine arrangement of the book. The means of communicating the message of Ruth and establishing the events upon the mind and heart of the reader is by dialogue. There are eighty-five verses in the book of Ruth; of these, fifty-eight are dialogue. These interesting dialogues, based mostly on question and answer form, are keys to unfold and impress the precious truth of this scriptural narrative.

The scene on the highway is one of unequaled tenderness. An insight is given into family relationships and family affection that would be a model for all time.

The first speaker in the book is Naomi. Her words spoken to Orpah and Ruth are revealing, *Go, return each to her mother's house. The Lord deal kindly with you, as ye have dealt with the dead, and me* (verse 8).

Naomi deeply appreciated the fidelity of Orpah and Ruth in their kindness to their husbands and also personally to herself. Purity and morality in marriage were evidences of faith in the only living God. These Moabitish damsels had lived in a sinful environment marked by unchaste and abominable idolatry. They had entered a home and family of Israelites where the law of God was honored, "Thou shalt not commit adultery" and "Thou shalt have no other gods." It is evident that they were influenced and, though of an evil race, had proved dutiful wives and kind daughters-in-law. Many have spoken of the failure of Mahlon and Chilion, but we have found no trace of the wicked ways of the evil world to be found in their lives. Naomi used the beautiful word "kindness" (Hebrew "Hesed"). Used again by Boaz concerning Ruth (chapter 3:10), it is a beautiful Hebrew reference to God's covenant love and grace to His people in the old testament times. David used the same expression when he said of Mephibosheth, "I will shew him kindness" (2 Samuel 9:1).

Naomi now is seen praying to the Lord on their behalf (verse 9). This touching insight into the character of Naomi is often passed

The Purposes of God

over. It reveals her deep concern for the blessing of marriage for her widowed daughters-in-law. She knew that in Moabitish society an unmarried woman's life and certainly a widow's life was one of great difficulty and disrespect. She loved her daughters-in-law and she had faith in the God of Israel who was living and caring. In this act of prayer she was acting in the Spirit who caused David to write, *Cast thy burden upon the Lord (Psalm 55:22)*. She desired the Lord to deal kindly with them. The burden of her prayer was that they might find a new home. We know that her prayer was answered abundantly in the resting place of Ruth in the home of Boaz, in which she herself had a welcome share. The prayer of the widow at the Bethlehem crossroads is an incentive to pray to the Lord, who loves to answer.

Thou art coming to a King.
Large petitions with thee bring
For His grace and power are such
None can ever ask too much

John Newton

Having concluded her prayer, *Naomi kissed them: and they lifted up their voice and wept (verse 9)*. The prospect of their beloved Naomi proceeding alone on her solitary way through life moved them both to reply in unison: *Surely we will return with thee unto thy people*. Although they were her daughters-in-law she loved them dearly and now addressed them as her daughters. Later it was said of Ruth that she was better than seven sons to Naomi (4:15). Naomi has now a delicate, difficult task in setting before them the costliness of their continuance in the pathway of companionship: The sad secret that, if they go with her, they may find no welcome, and the hope of a new husband and home is out of reach, as far as human resources appear.

Her own case is more distressful than theirs and it is most pain-

35

ful to part with them, for then she will be entirely alone. Had Naomi but considered, what she later clearly contemplated — the legal provisions with respect to levirate marriage — her depression and grief would have turned to joy. Lack of understanding the scripture was the cause of sadness for two men later on another highway walk in the sunset (Luke 24:17).

On three occasions in her conversation with Orpah and Ruth, Naomi insists on them going back to Moab (verses 11,12,15). Her question *Are there yet any sons in my womb, that they may be your husband?* would indicate that they understood the law of levirate marriage (Deuteronomy 25:5). This law was open to them as proselytes, but could not be fulfilled through Naomi, as she was beyond childbearing age. Even if she had a husband and sons, it would be folly to consider Ruth and Orpah waiting until they would be grown. Naomi was saddened by all these circumstances, but she acknowledged the sovereign ways of Jehovah in her deep afflictions and disclosed her faith in the covenant keeping God, in spite of all the outward distress of her position. Naomi's case was in the hand of Him from whom nothing is hidden—the One who cares! The beautiful words of William Cowper echo these thoughts of Naomi.

> Judge not the Lord by feeble sense
> But trust Him for His grace.
> Behind a frowning providence
> He hides a smiling face.

Naomi was testifying to the fact that Jehovah was intimately interested and active in the experiences of life.

A vital time has now been reached—the crisis at the crossroads. It will be a moment of revelation. The choice will affect the future of each, but especially Ruth. All must face choices through life which will determine their destiny, for better or worse. Such is the weighty lesson of the tale of these three widows on the highway.

Orpah and Ruth began to weep again. The issue at stake gave them great searching of heart, and trouble of spirit (verse 14). Orpah, like Ruth, is now faced by all that is entailed in continuing the journey to its end—all that it means in severing old ties, surrendering worldly prospects and in meeting unknown experiences in a strange land. Naomi has placed the issues faithfully before both of them, and each in turn must decide.

Orpah is the first to declare her choice. No spoken word of Orpah is recorded, but her final decision is made known by Naomi in the text: *Behold thy sister-in-law is gone unto her people, and unto her gods, return thou after thy sister-in-law (verse 14).*

Orpah kissed her mother in law. The Jews observe three kinds of kisses, which are acceptable; all others are wanton. There is the kiss of reverence to honor a person of dignity (1 Samuel 10:1); the second at the meeting of a friend (Exodus 4:27); a third at their parting, of which the kiss of Orpah is the given example. In contrast, to Orpah's taking leave of Naomi, Ruth clave unto her. This verb is the word which describes the faithful commitment of personal relationship. It is first indicated as used of the man for his wife in Eden (Genesis 2:24). Barnabas exhorted the believers at Antioch that with purpose of heart they would cleave unto the Lord (Acts 11:23). Ruth, a former idol worshipper, displayed by her clinging to Naomi, one of the features which Jehovah desired in His people. *Thou shalt fear the Lord thy God, to Him shalt thou cleave, and swear by His name... He is thy praise, and He is thy God (Deuteronomy 10:20,21).* This attitude of Ruth was the primary indication of her true confession of Jehovah's name and praise.

The life of Ruth had now reached its greatest moment. It was the time when the choice has to be made on which everything, as regards the divine purpose for her, must depend. What a crisis! How personal the confession she must make. Naomi again urged her to return. The path of faith was not an easy one for the Moabitess. She had moved step by step with Orpah, with whom she had accepted her Israelite husband, and who with her had bowed at the grave of widowhood. Orpah, with whom she had started on the way to Bethlehem, now is gone. In the light of reminiscence, she could recall her childhood home, her mother and father, the friendships of youth, and the scenes of Moab, once the center of all her interests. Before her lie the dark, forbidding hills of Israel, with its alien faces and unknown trials. What moves her to journey in the direction of another land? What calls her thither? It is a voice we cannot hear — the call of grace to a path of faith, hope and love. Alexander Whyte states that there is not a love story comparable to the love of Ruth towards Naomi. Her love for her aged mother in law is as pure gold and as strong as death. Many waters could not quench Ruth's love, nor floods drown her devotion. Her confession is the most beautiful expression of love in all the world's literature. The love of Ruth for Naomi was not merely natural affection; it was of a deep spiritual nature. She had fallen in love with Naomi's Lord, the God of Israel, under whose wings she had come to trust (chapter 2:12). The words by which she is remembered most are her open confession of faith, concerning her conversion to God, a happening which had transpired some time previously in the land of Moab. Her faith recalls Abraham, who, following his conversion as an idol worshipper, was called to go out into a place and went out, not knowing whither he went. Others confessed themselves strangers and pilgrims on the earth. If they had been mindful of that country from which they came, they might have had opportunity to return (Hebrews 11:8-16). Orpah went back to her gods and to her country and is mentioned no more in the scripture. We would seek to consider the most beautiful words of Ruth in which her resolve and desire is expressed in a most unhesitating confession of love. What a perfect carol of love begotten without a moment's effort. It is poetry which contains the deepest thoughts of a heart of love. This song tells where her great-grandson David received some of his talent to tune his lyre and sing Jehovah's praise.

Ruth commenced her wonderful confession of consecration with the words, Entreat me not to leave thee, or to return from following after thee. To her the word had come in power, as expressed in Psalm 45:10,11: *Hearken, O daughter, and consider, and incline thine ear; forget also thine own people, and thy father's house; So shall the King greatly desire thy beauty; for He is thy Lord; and worship thou Him.*

Ruth's decision is the young believer's model. How heaven must have rejoiced at her confession! It is still precious to God when a sinner turns to God from idols, drawn by cords of love, brought to Christ as Saviour, to publicly own Him, and confess Him as Lord. Here on the Bethlehem road we witness a pattern of wholehearted decision for the Lord. A soul thus delivered from sin can join with Robert Chapman and sing:

The cords that bound my heart to earth
are loosed by Jesus hand.
Before His cross I now am left
a stranger in the land.

Whither thou goest, I will go. Ruth had given up her home, her country and her gods, to follow Naomi. From henceforth her path will be determined by Naomi's path. Ittai, one of David's men, has his pathway determined by David. His words bear a striking resemblance to those of Ruth. *As the Lord liveth, surely in what place my Lord will be, whither in death or life, even there also will thy servant be (2 Samuel 15:21)*. For Ruth to enjoy the presence of Naomi she must tread the same path. It is so with the Christian. We have chosen the Saviour and our path must be determined by His. To have His company we must break from other by-paths. The Lord Jesus said to some, *Ye believe not because ye are not of My sheep, as I said unto you. My sheep hear My voice, and I know them, and they follow Me (John 10:26,27).* Oh, that all our readers could say, "I have chosen the Shepherd; whither thou goest, I will go."

Where thou lodgest, I will lodge. Ruth also chose places to lodge on the journey from the river Arnon, over the Jordan, along the winding and difficult way, until the final home is reached in Bethlehem-judah. So with us; this is not our home. This is not our place of resting; ours a city yet to come, onward to it, we are hasting, on to our eternal home. On the way to Bethlehem there were lodging places. Some may have been poor and despised, but there was sweet fellowship with Naomi, as well as the prospect of home.

Two disciples who had followed the Saviour in His path saw their need of a lodging place, and desired to lodge where His presence was known. *They said to Him, Where dwellest Thou? He answered, Come and see. So they came and saw where He dwelt and abode with Him that day, for it was about the tenth hour (John 1:38,39).* The lodging place illustrates and foreshadows the present day, for we have the privilege of being in the assembly fellowship of fellow-believers, who gather in the name of the Lord Jesus, and enjoy His person in the midst (Matthew 18:20). May true value be placed upon this lodging place on our spiritual journey home to heaven.

Thy people shall be my people. Ruth's choice of the people of God meant a new association. It was a most difficult choice to leave her father's house, her kindred and her land. How rewarding were the words of the kinsman-redeemer later: *Thou art come unto a people which thou knewest not heretofore... The Lord recompense thy work and a full reward be given thee of the Lord God of Israel, under whose wings thou art come to trust (Ruth 2:11,12).* Happy are all who identify openly and fully with the people of God, sharers of their privileges and responsibilities, like Moses who joined himself with the enslaved brickmakers in Egypt. He chose to suffer affliction with the people of God, rather than the pleasures and pomp of the palace of Egypt (Hebrews 11:24-26).

Thy God shall be my God. Ruth's renunciation of the gods of Moab involved separation. She turned to God from idols to serve the living and true God (1 Thessalonians 1:9). In the confession of Elohim, the name of God came from her lips; Ruth dethrones Chemosh forever and exalts Elohim as her future guide and shield. It was no mere human affection for Naomi which caused her true conversion and confession. She had fallen in love with Naomi's Lord, the God of Israel, under whose wings she had come to trust.

In this chapter the threefold name of God: El Shaddai, Jehovah, and Elohim, are interwoven into the three sections of the passage, as we have earlier shown. There are many names for God, for no one name could express all that He is, in Himself, and in His grace towards men. The name used here by Ruth is Elohim. This is the name used first in Genesis 1:1,2. It appears 2,550 time in the Old Testament. The meaning is simply God, as it is always rendered in the authorized version. The meaning of this name is clearly defined in its first mention. He is Supreme, Eternal; the Great Creator of all things. Campbell Morgan describes Elohim as the One to whom all power belongs, absolute, unqualified, unlimited energy. Elohim is also a plural noun, suggesting the truth of the Holy Trinity, which was fully revealed in the person and ministry of our Lord Jesus Christ. This One was the One chosen to be the God of Ruth. What wondrous grace had taught Ruth, the stranger brought up to worship the god of stone, Chemosh, to lift up her voice and heart to own allegiance to Elohim, her Creator and Saviour. *Thy God, my God.* These words are also the first utterance of the risen Christ: *I ascend to My Father, and your Father, to My God, and your God (John 20:17).* Wonderful nearness! Blessed relationship!

Where thou diest, will I die. Ruth expressed her steadfastness to continue in the pathway of faith even if it led to death. Her love was strong as death. She would follow to the end. Where did Christ die? At Calvary, upon the cross. There the believer dies also. *I am crucified with Christ (Galatians 2:20).* Do you accept that fact? Do you know its effect in your life?

O may I count myself to be
Dead to the sins that wounded thee,
Dead to the pleasures of this earth
Unworthy of my heavenly birth.

There will I be buried. Ruth is enrolled among the feminine worthies of faith in Israel, with Sarah, Rebekah, and Rachel. Her faith was expressed in her love. Friends desire to be buried with those whom they love. Barzillai expressed this desire to David: *Let me be buried by the grave of my father and mother (2 Samuel 19:37).*

To be buried with Christ is to realize that the last link with the old life is gone. Death dissolves the link. Burial hides the dead from sight. Baptism rightly understood is the symbol of the union. "There will I be buried." Where was he buried? In the garden tomb!

Back to the cross I look and wondering see,
The Christ of God in agony for me.
But gazing on that form divine
I see with Him myself - His death is mine.

Again beside the garden tomb I stand
And watch Him buried there with reverent hand.
But in that grave faith sees not one, but two.
God hid me there forever from His view.

If ought but death part thee from me. Ruth accepted the fact that death would part her from Naomi, as far as this life was concerned, but she would live with Naomi all through her life. In the course of things Naomi, now old, was given the comforting assurance of the care and kindness of Ruth always. The expectation of death was the final goal of life for these saints of Old Testament times. As present day saints we have a blessed hope.

We are not looking for death, but for the coming again of the Lord Jesus to receive us unto Himself without dying (John 14:1-3). Ruth turned to God from idols, to serve the living and true God. All believers in this age can add the words which were not true of Ruth - to wait for His Son from heaven. What a hope! When? Perhaps today! Ruth had a plan for her future, "to live and die by faith." This commitment of fidelity she sealed with a solemn oath. "The Lord do so to me and more also" is an expression of her faith in the living God of Naomi, and her God also, in whose name she vows to fulfill her confession, calling His judgment upon her should she fail.

When Naomi saw that she was steadfastly minded to go with her, she had no further words to speak. Nothing more could be said. Are we steadfastly minded to continue in the path of pilgrim faith? It is only constraining love that will lead us to make that choice.

I have seen the face of Jesus.
Tell me naught of aught beside
I have heard the voice of Jesus
And my heart is satisfied.

It was so with Ruth; she had made her choice. Henceforth her life was to be bound up in the bundle of life with the people of God (1 Samuel 25:29).

III. THE GOD OF GRACE: JEHOVAH

The earlier verses of this great chapter have traced events which marked the commencement of the journey to Bethlehem and choices at the crossroad. The closing verses trace continuance of that journey and arrival there.

So they two went until they came to Bethlehem. (1:19)

These words are in sharp contrast to the opening verses of the chapter where two couples, a man and his wife, and two sons, are seen on a journey away from Bethlehem to escape a famine. Three of them never returned. Here one who had gone is returning and a newcomer to the Bethlehem highway walks by her side. God has visited His people in Bethlehem, giving bread, and has caused the good news to reach the far country. With their faces towards God's land, and God's people, the restored saint and the newly converted soul press on *until they came to Bethlehem*.

The road from Moab to Judah is a long, difficult way, beset with storms, desolate mountain paths and the added danger of thieves. The time taken and hardships endured we can only speculate. Naomi was recalling her sorrows since leaving Bethlehem. What thoughts must have filled her heart as she remembered the journey with Elimelech, her husband, and her two sons, on their way down to Moab. They were removed by God, and she was spared by His goodness.

What a vivid picture of what Paul describes as *the goodness and severity of God (Romans 11:22)*. We behold God's severity in cutting them off and His goodness in sparing Naomi. This government and goodness of Jehovah are also linked with His grace as seen in Ruth (chapter 2:10).

ARRIVAL AT BETHLEHEM

They came to Bethlehem. And it came to pass when they were come to Bethlehem, that all the city was moved about them. And they said, is this Naomi? And she said unto them, call me not Naomi, call me Mara, for the Almighty hath dealt very bitterly with me. I went out full, and the Lord hath brought me home again empty; why then call ye me Naomi, seeing the Lord hath testified against me and the Almighty hath afflicted me? So Naomi returned, and Ruth the Moabitess, the daughter-in-law with her, which returned out of the land of Moab, and they came to Bethlehem in the beginning of barley harvest. (1:19-22)

After the long absence of more than ten years, Naomi returned to Bethlehem, and Ruth the Moabitess with her. There was a great commotion in the city at their arrival. Some perhaps were moved with gladness, others with sadness to see Naomi return without her husband and sons. Likely some would view her with mixed feelings because of her past unfaithfulness in wandering away from God's people to sojourn among Israel's enemies. Her arrival had aroused the curiosity of Bethlehem. This chapter is for the most part female in character; all the dialogues are between women. On this occasion the town of Bethlehem speaks to the returning widow in the voice of its women.

The apparent change caused by her depression and grief was expressed in her appearance. Those who did recognize her asked the question "Is this Naomi?" In her answer the play on her name becomes evident: "Call me not Naomi, which means pleasantness, but call me rather Mara, which means bitterness." Whatever emotions moved the women of Bethlehem, Naomi was moved by her sense of failure. She confessed that El Shaddai had a right to deal with her, for she had gone out full, but she also deeply appreciated that Jehovah had brought her home again. Naomi experienced the truth of the remarkable words written hundreds of years later: *Now no chastening for the present seemeth to be joyous, but grievous - nevertheless afterward it yieldeth the peaceable fruit of righteousness unto them which are exercised thereby (Hebrews 12:11).*

The names of God used in this magnificent chapter reveal His character and purposes toward His people. As El Shaddai (chapter 1:21) He is almighty and all sufficient; as Elohim (chapter 1:16) He is the Triune God of all power. Jehovah is named seven times (chapter 1:8, 9, 13, 17, 21) He that is, that was, and that is to come; the Everlasting One. This name is above every other name of God. To every Jew it is the one most precious, and the most revealing of His grace towards His people. According to lexicographers it is the most frequently used, occurring 6,823 times. Recurring seven times in this chapter, it is well suited to describe the God of grace whose covenant name, Jehovah, contained within itself the pledge of all that He had promised to do for them and to be to them. Naomi feared Him as the One who chastised for wrongdoing, but trusted Him as her shield and defender when restored. The gradual unfolding of His will and purposes, and grace, gave to Naomi a new meaning of Jehovah's name. To Christians it is delightful to recognize in Jesus, whose precious name is "Jehovah the Saviour" (Matthew 1:21), the same Jehovah of the Old Testament. He declared Himself to be the "I AM." The Lord Jesus is the living One, who in wondrous grace became dead, for our salvation, but who is alive forever more (Revelation 1:18). He is eternal, our Redeemer and unchangeable Lord. We rejoice to affirm that Jehovah, rendered Lord, in capital letters in the Authorized Version of the Old Testament, is the Lord Jesus revealed in the New Testament.

The words of the beautiful poem, "The Weaver," are the epitome of Jehovah's dealings with Naomi.

Not till the loom is silent
And the shuttles cease to fly,
Will God unroll the canvas
And explain the reason why
The dark threads were as needful
In the weaver's skillful hand
As the threads of gold and silver
In the pattern He had planned.

The last verse ends with an indication of hope. It is a link between scenes of distress and scenes of delight. Naomi had left Bethlehem because of famine. Now she returns to fields of barley harvest. She returned, not empty handed, as she supposed, for the Divine Author adds: *And Ruth, the Moabitess, her daughter-in-law, with her, which returned out of the country of Moab.*

None of the women had taken notice of Ruth. She was of little account to them. The whole city was moved at Naomi's return, but no one seems to be concerned for Ruth. Now Naomi is left alone save for "Ruth the Moabitess" as the sacred historian describes her, to show the tenderness of the stranger from a heathen land and the indifference of the pious Hebrews of Bethlehem. The designation "Ruth the Moabitess" is used five times of Ruth (chapter 1:22, chapter 2:2, 21, and chapter 4:5,10). The Spirit of God underscores this fact for a divine purpose. In Deuteronomy 23:3, it is plainly stated that a Moabite shall not enter into the congregation of the Lord even to the tenth generation. How then was it possible for Ruth to be brought in? The usual explanation is that grace abounded, and God overruled His former law. It should be carefully noted, however, that Moabite (Deuteronomy 23:3) is in the Hebrew text; masculine, therefore Ruth was not excluded from the congregation. Five times she is called "Ruth the Moabitess" and once "the Moabitess damsel." The Spirit impresses this important fact. A long list of nations were forbidden to be taken in marriage by God's people, but an exception is made in the omission of the Moabites (Deuteronomy 7:1-3). We conclude that Boaz was within his rights as a pious Israelite to take Ruth, whom he himself described as the Moabitess, to be his wife. In this we see the harmony and beauty of the scriptures to foresee and provide for Ruth to have her place in Judah's royal line, through whom the Messiah of Israel, our Lord Jesus Christ, would come into the world (Micah 5:2).

The final sentence states the time of the arrival of Naomi and Ruth was in the beginning of barley harvest. They had arrived at the right place, and they came at a good time. The barley harvest was the early springtime, the barley being the first of the ripened grain (Exodus 9:31,32), the first fruits of the earth, to be followed by the wheat and vintage. It was a time of joy. Those who shared in the barley harvest were in good time to enjoy the blessings of the entire time of gathering of the fruits of the earth.

In order to understand some of the spiritual significance of the term "beginning of barley harvest," reference must be made to "The Feasts of Jehovah" (Leviticus 23). Each of the seven feasts corresponds with some particular aspects of the person and work of the Lord Jesus Christ. A brief outline of these will enhance the distinct message of the term "barley harvest."

1. **The Feast of Passover** (Leviticus 23:5). This finds its fulfillment in the death of Christ. "Christ our Passover" (1 Corinthians 5:7) observed on the 14th day of the 1st month in the evening.

2. **The Feast of Unleavened Bread** (Leviticus 23:6). This followed immediately and was observed for seven days, beginning on the 15th day of the month. It finds its complete fulfillment in the holy walk of the Lord's people as they feed on Christ, the Bread of Life (1 Corinthians 5:6).

3. **The Feast of the Firstfruits** (Leviticus 23:11). This was observed "on the morrow after the Sabbath," that is, three days after the

Passover, upon the first day of the week. It is a remarkable type of the Resurrection of Christ from the dead. He is indeed the firstfruits of them that slept (1 Corinthians 15:20).

4. **The Feast of Pentecost** (Leviticus 23:15,16). This feast finds its fulfillment in the descent of the Holy Spirit (Acts 2:1). Pentecost means fiftieth. It was exactly 50 days after Christ's Resurrection that the Spirit came. The Book of Ruth is the special book read by the Jews at Pentecost.

5. **The Feast of Trumpets** (Leviticus 23:24). This memorial blowing of trumpets gathered the people to worship Jehovah. Before Christ returns to be worshipped as King of Kings, Israel will be re-gathered, and then this feast will be fulfilled.

6. **The Day of Atonement** (Leviticus 23:27). This was a time of mourning, and points on to that day when Israel will look on Him whom they pierced (Zechariah 12:10). It is the time of repentance and restoration of the nation of Israel.

7. **The Feast of Tabernacles** (Leviticus 23:34). This is a time of rejoicing and points to the millennial reign of our Blessed Lord, over Israel and the whole universe. Thus, the beginning of barley harvest suggests, spiritually, the blessings coming to the Lord's people from the death and subsequent resurrection of Christ. So Naomi and Ruth came home at the "joy of harvest" to share the blessings of the people of God. Christ is risen and from Him flow the blessings of God to His saints. As we read this beautiful gem of literature may we enjoy some "handfuls on purpose" (chapter 2:16).

The Mighty Man of Wealth: Boaz - Type of Christ

Jesus saw me when a stranger
And He kindly welcomed me.
In His eyes I find such favor,
Wondrous grace! How can it be?

Now no longer I'm a stranger
By His precious blood made nigh;
Neath His wings I fear no danger
He doth all my need supply.

Gleaning in His field till even,
At His feet till morn I'll lie;
Precious promises receiving,
While redemption draweth nigh.

O the grace of my Redeemer,
Mighty Man of wealth was He;
Sold His all to win the stranger;
His own self He gave for me.

He is precious, my Redeemer,
Chiefest of ten thousand He;
All my praise to Him I render,
Now and through eternity.

From Words in Season - 1941, Author Unknown

The Provisions of God

The second chapter of Ruth enlarges upon the provision envisaged by the beginning of the barley harvest in Chapter 1:22. The two widows in great need arrived in Bethlehem (house of bread) at the very time when the barley harvest was ready for reaping. Harvest time is always a season of great joy, and of spiritual importance in the scriptures. The barley harvest was the prelude to the "Joy of Harvest" (Isaiah 9:3). It introduced the blessing of the entire ingathering of the grain and vintage. In the first chapter Ruth is seen as a stranger to God, yet turning to God from idols, in wholehearted allegiance and determined resolve. What a demonstration of devotion! Here in this delightful chapter Ruth is a gleaner of God's provision for the stranger and the poor. We admire her diligence in going into the harvest field in humility to appropriate what grace has given. What a display of faith!

Three important sections develop the main themes of this beautiful portion of God's Word: I. **The presentation of the Redeemer** (verses 1-4); II. **The prosperity of the field** (verses 5-16); III. **The progress of the stranger** (verses 17-23).

1. THE PRESENTATION OF THE REDEEMER

And Naomi had a kinsman of her husband's, a mighty man of wealth, of the family of Elimelech; and his name was Boaz. And Ruth the Moabitess said unto Naomi, Let me now go to the field, and glean ears of corn after him in whose eyes I shall find grace. And she said unto her, Go my daughter. And she went, and came, and gleaned in the field after the reapers; And her hap was to light on a part of the field belonging unto Boaz, who was of the kindred of Elimelech. And, behold, Boaz came from Bethlehem, and said unto the reapers, The Lord be with you: And they answered him, The Lord bless thee. (2:1-4)

We are sure that the Holy Spirit, whose divine mission is to glorify and testify of the Lord Jesus Christ (John 15:26), points in the pen picture of Boaz to the great antitype Christ Himself. As a foreshadowing of Christ the Redeemer, Boaz is a striking instance of prevision. On the evening of the resurrection day our Lord Jesus expounded to two disciples on the way to Emmaus "things concerning Himself" from Moses, and all the prophets. As a result, the two disciples testified, *Did not our heart burn within us while He talked with us by the way, and while He opened to us the scriptures?* (*Luke 24:27-32*). In such a Bible reading the subject of redemption would have an important place, as it is the grand theme of the entire scriptures. The Book of Ruth supplies one of the great keys to illustrate the work of the Redeemer, so doubtless was included in the things concerning Himself. Redemption is the act of buying back, and then taking possession of that which has been purchased. The pictures point to a redemption procured by paying a price, and also by the putting forth of power. The fulfillment in the New Testament indicates redemption by blood, which the believer presently enjoys (Ephesians 1:7), but also redemption by power which is the hope of the saints when the Redeemer returns (Ephesians 4:30). This was evident in the redemption of Israel. They were redeemed by the blood of the lamb from judgment, and by the power of the arm of the Lord from Pharaoh and his hosts. God's purpose was to have them as His peculiar people, to dwell in their midst, and receive their service, worship, obedience and love.

It is interesting to consider that the events of this chapter occurred at Bethlehem, and that the focal point is the field. The place is ever precious as the birthplace of Immanuel, the Redeemer. In the field where gleaners gathered sheaves, shepherds later watched their flock. The time factor is also important as pointing forward to the glorious purpose for which He came into the world; Ruth came to Bethlehem at the Passover; the season of His death, burial and resurrection. The time of harvest ended after seven weeks, during which Ruth continued to glean and dwell with Naomi (chapter 2:23). Pentecost, meaning fiftieth, took place fifty days after the waving of the sheaf of the first fruits. It is an important time in God's calendar. The Lord Jesus honored Bethlehem by His birth, He also honored the Passover by becoming the Paschal Lamb on the very day of the feast. The Father honored His Son by raising Him from the dead on the very day that the sheaf of the first fruits was waved before the Lord. *And when the day of Pentecost was fully come* (fulfilled) (*Acts 2:1*) - fifty days after the Resurrection of Christ - the Holy Spirit honored that day by descending in great power. It was the birthday of the Church of this age.

The exact fulfillment of these types, even unto the very day, could not have been mere chance. On the contrary, it reveals how marvelously God had foretold His great purpose and plan through these "shadows of things to come." It is therefore in keeping with the wonderful type of the Person of Christ illustrated in Boaz in this magnificent chapter, that there should be in its background a cluster of graphic foreshadowings of the redeeming work of Christ, His glorious resurrection, and ascension, and the consequent coming of the Person of the Holy Spirit.

Consider Boaz as he suggests Christ in at least seven ways in this chapter:

1. **A friend of the poor** (verse 1) — The word kinsman in this verse is not the one used twelve times elsewhere in the book, where it is the *go'el*, one who hath the right to redeem, but rather simply a friend. He was a friend who became closer than a brother. Surely in this we see the sinner's Friend, even Christ (Luke 7:34).

2. **A mighty man of wealth** (verse 1) — These opening descriptive glimpses of Boaz are to inform the reader of the abilities of the one who will be the most important in the story of Ruth. He prefigures in his wealth the Lord Jesus, the glorified One in heaven, whose unsearchable riches were preached among the Gentiles by Paul (Ephesians 3:8).

3. **The power of his name; Boaz**– *in him is strength*. — The Risen Lord said, *All power is given unto Me in heaven and on earth (Matthew 28:18)*. In memorial of his honorable ancestor, Solomon named one of the pillars of the temple Boaz, which signified strength. We know it was given to him in writing from his father David, who had received the instruction from the Lord (1 Chronicles 28:19). God rewarded Boaz, who overcame the testings of the famine, and kept the Word of God, and had strength, insomuch that this pillar in the temple honored his faithfulness. The one who overcometh in our age will be made a pillar in the temple of God (Revelation 3:12).

4. **The Lord of the harvest** (verse 4) — In the midst of the field Boaz was lord of the harvest. He was a gracious master having contented workers. He was moved with compassion as he saw the widow and the poor in the field. Of the Greater than Boaz we read: *When He saw the multitudes He was moved with compassion...and He said, The harvest truly is plenteous, but the laborers are few. Pray ye*

therefore the Lord of the harvest, that He will send forth laborers into His harvest (Matthew 9:36-38).

5. **A man in whose heart was God's Word** (Deuteronomy 24:19) — God made merciful provision in His Word for the stranger, and for the widow, *When thou cuttest down thy harvest in thy field, and hath forgot a sheaf in the field, thou shalt not go again to fetch it. It shall be for the stranger, and for the widow, that the Lord thy God may bless thee in all the work of thy hands (Deuteronomy 24:19).* In the days when Boaz lived every man did that which was right in his own eyes. It is likely his was the only field where handfuls on purpose were especially dropped in the path of strangers and widows. In this desire to follow the Word of God in providing for the destitute we perceive likeness to Him who said, *It is more blessed to give than to receive (Acts 20:35),* which words we are exhorted to remember.

6. **A man whose lips were full of grace** (verse 10) — The gracious words of Boaz fell with encouragement on the ears of Ruth. Naomi had not spoken any words like these. Ruth confessed that his words had comforted her and that he had spoken to her heart, though she acknowledged she was unworthy. No other had ever displayed such grace. Never man spake like this man. Bible lovers perceive in the gracious ministry of Boaz foregleams of Him, Who when He spake all eyes were turned to see the Speaker and marveled at the words which proceeded out of His mouth.

Replenished are thy lips with grace
and full of love thy tender heart.
Charles Wesley

These presentations of Boaz, in the book bearing his bride's name - lord of the harvest, friend of the poor, man of wealth, wisdom, words and witness - foreshadow the Greater than Boaz, Christ

Himself, in every facet of the character of Boaz. However, in Boaz as the go'el, the most expressive type of Christ is foreshadowed.

7. **One who had the right of redemption** (verse 20 R.V.) — Under God's law, a kinsman was invested with a right to redeem (Leviticus 25:25). Redemption is one of the grand themes of scripture; its scarlet thread is the royal subject of the entire book.

A survey of the whole Bible in relationship to redemption, the Redeemer, and the redeemed is a fascinating study, yielding bread to the eater, seed to the sower, and a full basket to a worshipper. A broad outline could be tabulated as follows: The Divine Intention expressed — foreshadowed in the Pentateuch (Exodus 12); the Divine Illustration exemplified — foreseen in the histories (Ruth 4); the Divine Intimation envisaged — foretold in the Prophecies (Isaiah 44:24, 59:20); the Divine Ideal exalted — factual in the Gospels (Luke 1:68); the Divine Indispensable emphasized — fruitful in the Epistles (1 Peter 1:18-21); the Divine Invitation extended — fulfilled in the Revelation (Revelation 19:6-9).

The Hebrew word go'el for redeemer is also translated "kinsman" and "avenger." The essentials in redemption under the law were important. The redeemer must be near of kin to the one in need. The right of relationship must be established. Boaz had this right. We have in the Lord Jesus One who took on Him the seed of Abraham, and was made of a woman to redeem (Hebrews 2:16, Galatians 4:4). He became our Kinsman by His incarnation. He became a true and perfect man, sinless and impeccable. This truth must be jealously guarded and reverently believed. The Lord Jesus was verily God, yet became truly human in order to obtain eternal redemption.

The claimant of relationship must possess suitable resources to pay the sum demanded. Boaz was a man who had adequate capital. Of our Lord Jesus it is written, "It was exacted and He became answerable." This rendering given by Bishop Lowth is valuable.

The kinsman must also have a willingness and a determined resolve to redeem. What Boaz purposed in his heart was willingly expressed in his words, *Ye are witnesses – I have bought all. Of our Blessed Lord it is written, He selleth all that He had and buyeth that field,* also, *When He had found one pearl of great price, went and sold all that He had, and bought it (Matthew 13:44,46).*

As we trace the Hebrew law of redemption, an outline of its demands and responsibilities appear to be:

1. When a person had lost his property, by adversity or the death of a husband, it could be restored through one who was near of kin.

2. Certain demands imposed legally must be met. This aspect is often referred to as avenging, or as better understood doing justice. The widow's plea was *Avenge me of mine adversary (Luke 18:3).* Mr. Newberry translates, "Do me justice from my legal opponent."

3. The redemptive price determined by the law must be fully paid. A document as evidence of the purchase being completed, signed by competent witnesses, must be drawn up and sealed (Jeremiah 32:9-11).

4. Finally, the widow in her adversity had a claim upon the kinsman, who, if single, was responsible to take the widow as his wife (Deuteronomy 25:5-10).

Therefore, this God-given law had great significance, as the function of the go'el held the prerogatives of redemption, and the kinsman-avenger-redeemer also became the bridegroom. These four functions as seen in our Lord Jesus Christ should be studied in the beautiful illustration supplied by the relationship of Boaz with Ruth. The kinsman was obligated to prove his right, vindicate the law, pay the debt and complete a union. Concerning the Lord as the Go'el, the redeemed shall forever sing, *Thou art worthy...for Thou wast slain, and hast redeemed us to God by Thy blood (Revelation 5:9).*

Jesus is worthy to receive
Honor and power Divine,
And blessings more than we can give
Be, Lord forever Thine

Isaac Watts

And Ruth said to Naomi, Let me now go to the field, and glean ears of corn after him in whose sight I shall find grace. And she said unto her, Go, my daughter. And she went, and came, and gleaned in the field after the reapers, and her hap was to light on a part of the field belonging unto Boaz. (2:2,3)

Ruth had some knowledge of the gracious provision God had ordained for the stranger, the widow and the fatherless, in the time of harvest. God, Who caused fruitful seasons, desired that His people would consider the destitute and hungry. The corners of this field were not to be wholly reaped, nor all the gleanings of the field to be taken home (Leviticus 19:9). Ruth knew that, to sustain life, this was an open door for her, as she was a stranger, a widow, and likely fatherless also. She thought of Naomi, now too weak and aged to work in the harvest field; thus she went out in humility, asking for permission to join the poor, who were appointed the lowest place in the field of the mighty man of wealth. Ruth was satisfied as a gleaner among the outcasts of Israel. The guidance of God is one of the great keys in the Book of Ruth. The expression "her hap was to light on a part of the field belonging to Boaz," is not to be taken as a chance happening. She was guided by the God of Israel, under Whose wings she had come to trust. It was so with Moses (Exodus 3:1) whose call came also as he was at his daily toil.

In this brief beginning of Ruth's service in the field, many spiritual lessons are evident. Ruth is a picture of a young believer. She was in a strange land. Her actions outline the spiritual conduct of one newly come to the faith. Her attitude of care for others, lowliness, diligence, obedience and thankfulness is an excellent role model for new converts. As a gleaner she is a picture of a newborn soul, going forth into the fields of scripture, to gather food for the new life. It was not sufficient to make the right choice in confessing faith in the Lord; Ruth needed food to sustain her in the land.

Boaz came from Bethlehem to survey the harvesting and the workers. The lord of the harvest enters his field with a prayer for his own: "The Lord be with you." The response of the field was: "The Lord bless thee."

This address, with the response, is one of the first examples of prayer and benediction in the work place. David, who dwelt later in these fields of Bethlehem, wrote words based on the words of Boaz, his great grandfather. In a picture of famine conditions he wrote: *Let them be as grass upon the housetops, which withereth afore it groweth up, wherewith the mower filleth not his hand: nor he that bindeth sheaves his bosom. Neither do they which go by say: The blessings of the Lord be upon thee: We bless you in the Name of the Lord* (Psalm 129:6-8).

A contrast is seen in this Psalm to the delightful scenes of prosperity in the harvest field of Boaz. In the first there is a beautiful dispensational foreshadowing of the millennial reign of Christ, a scene of peace and prosperity. *In those days they shall beat their swords into plowshares, and their spears into pruning hooks: nation shall not lift up sword against nation, neither shall they learn war anymore* (Isaiah 2:4). Instead of instruments of destruction men will devise greater equipment to harvest the abundant grain, when the earth shall yield its increase. Even a handful of corn upon a mountain top will produce a harvest during the glorious dominion of Christ. The existence of management and labor in happy relationship and contentment in the employ of Boaz is a delightful prevision of earth's golden age (Psalm 72).

The warm greeting exchanged between Boaz and his men showed their devotion to the Lord, their faith in God, and their dwelling together in unity. It is a good and pleasant sight, and a condition that brings the blessing of Jehovah (Psalm 133), under whose wings thou art come to trust (Ruth 2:21) — the shadowing wings:

Within the rest of Thine All-Shadowing Wing.
Hide, Hide Thou Me,
That I may some small note or music bring,
Of joy to Thee.

Ah, There is blended with this one small chord
A note divine:
Thy love has purchased me, O risen Lord,
And made me Thine.

Yea, 'twas Thy love to me that made me love,
And loving sing,
Sweet love that loves to love so far above
All I can bring.

'Tis but a little note thou givest me,
Breathed from above,
That I may give it back again to Thee,
Thou God of love.

S. Trevor Francis

II. THE PROSPERITY OF THE FIELD

The days of the judges were times of great manifestations of Satan's power, man's lawlessness and departure from God. Many disorders were evident in other parcels of ground that made up the fields of Bethlehem. There were landmarks, but no signs to identify ownership. Ruth was guided to a special part of the field. In many ways the field of Boaz is a true picture of a New Testament church. Paul used such an illustration when he described the local assembly at Corinth as God's cultivated field (1 Corinthians 3:6-9). He used the idea of planting as the initial gospel work, watering as the ministry of the word, ascribing all blessings to God who gives the increase. He indicates that all who serve in any way are laborers together, and every one shall receive his own reward according to his own labor.

Some features of the field of Boaz are instructive. He was lord of the field. This field belonged to one person; it was his own field. All his interests were there, his servants in their diverse labors were under his control. He was supreme, his name was above all others. A New Testament assembly is a place in a world of lawlessness where the Lordship of Christ is acknowledged, and His name honored.

THE NAMELESS SERVANT OVER THE FIELD

Then said Boaz unto his servant, that was set over the reapers, whose damsel is this? And the servant that was over the reapers Answered and said, It is the Moabitish damsel that came back with Naomi out of the country of Moab: And she said I pray you, let me glean and gather after the reapers among the sheaves: So she came and hath continued even from the morning until now, that she tarried a little in the house. (2:5-7)

This servant who is mentioned twice is unnamed, and is a valuable illustration of the Holy Spirit of God.

Seven men in the Old Testament, all of whom are pictures of the Holy Spirit in various aspects of His work, are nameless. A brief consideration of these are windows to shed light on the many facets of the gracious ministry of the Person of the Holy Spirit of God.

1. **Abraham's Servant** — *And the servant took Rebekah, and went his way.... And the servant said, It is my master....And the servant told Isaac all things that he had done (Genesis 24:61,65,66).*

The servant who convinced her concerning the person of one whom she had not seen, by word alone, became the comforter who came alongside to conduct her on the pilgrimage to the one, whom having not seen, she loved. What a beautiful illustration of the Saviour's promise concerning "The Comforter" even "The Spirit of Truth" (John 14:16,17).

2. **Joseph's servant** — *And they knew not that Joseph understood them: for he spake unto them by an interpreter (Genesis 42:23).* The Holy Spirit is the one who interprets the words of Christ, guiding the saints into the understanding of all truth and showing them things to come (John 14:15-26, 16:12-13).

3. **Jesse's servant** — *And Samuel said: are here all thy children? and Jesse said, There remaineth yet the youngest, and behold he keepeth the sheep, and Samuel said unto Jesse, Send and fetch him, for we will not sit around till he come hither; and he sent a nameless servant who brought him unto the central place* (1 Samuel 16:11,12). No circle is complete without the person of our Lord Jesus. It is the objective of the Holy Spirit to bring Christ into preeminence, hence the Lord Jesus said of Him: *He shall glorify me* (John 16:14).

4. **Saul's servant** — *Then answered one of the servants and said, Behold I have seen a son of Jesse, that is cunning in playing, a mighty valiant man, and a man skilful in matters, and a man of war, and a comely person, and the Lord is with him* (1 Samuel 16:18). There was no mistaking the identity of such a one as this - he was fairer than all the other sons - *so Saul sent messengers unto Jesse and said, Send me David thy son, who is the shepherd* (1 Samuel 16:19).

This servant exalted the Lord's anointed, The greater than David said of the Holy Spirit "He shall testify of me" (John 15:26).

5. **David's servant** — *And David rose up early in the morning, and left the sheep with a keeper... Eliab said, With whom hast thou left those few sheep in the wilderness (1 Samuel 17:20,28)?*

During David's absence he had provided for the care of the sheep, in the wilderness. During the absence of Christ in Heaven, He has not left His own sheep to tread life's pathway alone on earth. He, the Great Shepherd of His chosen flock, has left them in the hand of the Keeper, which is the Holy Spirit. Indeed his promise was that His glorification was essential in order that the Spirit should come and reside among His people until His coming again (John 14:18, 16:7).

6. **Saul's servant** — *And David left 'the food supply (baggage) in the hand of the keeper (1 Samuel 17:22).* After Israel and its king had been fully tested for forty days, David was sent forth from the father and came to them from Bethlehem, the House of Bread, laden with an ephah of parched corn, ten loaves, and ten cheeses. All these he placed in the charge of the keeper, till he himself would meet the foe and triumph gloriously. Then only could the blessings from the father through the son be appreciated.

All this is a faint picture of the words of the Saviour before He endured the conflict upon the cross, when he said, *I have yet many things to say unto you but ye cannot bear them now (John 16:12).* However He promised that the Holy Spirit would bring all things to their remembrance, whatsoever He had said. He would also guide them into all truth, and bring before them things to come (John 16:13).

Bethlehem after Calvary would yield royal dainties to be unfolded by the Holy Spirit in the giving of the four Gospels, the Acts, the Epistles, and the Revelation (John 14:26, 16:13).

7. **Boaz's servant** — The servant of Boaz *was set over the reapers (Ruth 2:6).* He was the one who divided to every man his appointed place, interviewed newcomers to the field and looked after the interest of the Lord of the harvest.

So the person of the Holy Spirit is here today to oversee the interests of Christ in the field of testimony. The Holy Spirit is the Lord, the Spirit (2 Corinthians 3:18 R.V.).

In these nameless servants a wonderful unfolding of the work of the person of the Holy Spirit is presented: as the One who comes alongside His people in their pilgrimage, the interpreter of God's Word, the One who testifies and glorifies Christ, who cares for the flock and supplies food for the soul, and who is also the overseer of divine testimony on earth.

The eyes of Boaz in surveying his field became aware of the newcomer. His interest was aroused so he enquired of his steward, "Whose damsel is this?" The servant was able to tell his master who the stranger was. He was conversant with her background and was able to give a very complimentary outline of her humble entrance to the field, her diligent gleaning during the morning and the period of resting for a little while in the shelter provided for workers. What an example of a godly overseer! If someone were to enquire concerning one newly come to the faith, could an account be given as those who watch for their souls and care for the flock? Do we know the backgrounds and spiritual histories of the lambs?

Boaz, the man of wealth, the lord of the harvest, upon hearing the good testimony of the Moabitess stranger, turned to give her welcome as a gleaner. What grace filled his heart and how sweet to her ears must have been the first words with which he addressed her! In the record these are the first words of encouragement her ears had heard. The master had taken notice of her, when others passed her by, and had called her by the tender name of daughter. She had truly found what she had longed for as she set out in the morning, someone who would show her grace. The overruling of God is exemplified in guiding Ruth to the field of Boaz, and bringing Boaz to visit the field at an hour when she was present. When our lives are under divine control, what transpires is no mere accident but heaven's arrangement. By addressing Ruth as "my daughter" reference to the age difference was indicated, but it was also no doubt a word of endearment.

BOAZ SPEAKS TO RUTH

Then said Boaz unto Ruth, Hearest thou not my daughter? Go not to glean in another field, neither go from hence, but abide here fast by my maidens. Let thine eye be on the field that they do reap, and go thou after them. Have I not charged the young men that they shall not touch thee? And when thou art athirst, go unto the vessels and drink of that which the young men have drawn. (2:8,9)

In these instructions, Ruth was granted special provision and protection, promised by Boaz himself. How sweet and cheering must have been his first words to her heart! He had conveyed to her the precious truth of her acceptance into the field with all its privileges and also all its responsibilities. The stranger from afar is welcomed into the circle of fellowship. He has given instructions to the young men to protect her and to provide for her, and the young women to bring her into a place where she would have easy access to the best of the gleanings. When she was thirsty, others would draw water for her. Boaz was providing for her far beyond the required dictates of the law. Truly, grace was abounding.

Having designed her place of service, he has made known his care in all his provisions for her comfort and blessing as a stranger in the new sphere of fellowship. It is all richly suggestive of the place where believers enjoy such mutual consideration when acting in submission to the Lord Himself, even a local assembly of God.

As strangers we have been guided to the place where the Word of God is honoured, all its precepts owned, where the Lordship of Christ is seen, where the Holy Spirit presides and where service is appointed. There, while we enjoy God's presence, it has been clearly shown to us that our fellowship must be a separated one. Boaz encouraged Ruth to continue gleaning in his field and to keep company with his maidens. It would have been easy to drift to other areas that seemed attractive, but where only parts of the Word of God were owned and where departure from God's principles was evident.

RUTH'S RESPONSE

Then she fell on her face, and bowed herself to the ground, and said unto him, Why have I found grace in thine eyes, that thou shouldest take knowledge of me, seeing I am a stranger? (2:10)

The response of Ruth was made in great humility. She bowed before Boaz with her face to the earth. For similar acts of prostration to show reverence and appreciation, according to the Eastern custom, see such passages as Genesis 19:1; Joshua 5:14; 1 Samuel 25:23,24 and 2 Samuel 1:2.

Ruth realized the favor she had found in the sight of Boaz and thus took a place of true adoration. This same attitude marked Abigail who also, in a day still future, bowed herself on her face to the earth at the message of David, wondering at his grace and favour (1 Samuel 25:41,42). Every saint may say with wonder in the words of Judas (not Iscariot), *Lord, how is it that thou wilt manifest Thyself unto us and not unto the world* (John 14:22). This great question of Ruth, *Why have I found grace in thine eyes, that thou shouldest take knowledge of me, seeing I am a stranger?* has an echo in the heart of all the redeemed. We can rightly express our adoration for grace in the words of Isaac Watts:

Why was I made to hear His voice
And enter while there's room,

When thousands make a wretched choice,
And rather starve than come.

'Twas the same grace that spread the feast
That sweetly drew me in,
Else I would still refuse to come,
And perish in my sin.

BOAZ SPEAKS TO RUTH

And Boaz answered and said unto her, It hath fully been shewed me, all that thou hast done unto thy mother in law, since the death of thy husband: And how thou hast left thy father and thy mother, and the land of thy nativity, and art come unto a people which thou knewest not heretofore. The Lord recompense thy work, and a full reward be given thee of the Lord God of Israel, under whose wings thou art come to trust (take refuge R.V.). (2:11,12)

The answer of Boaz is not simply that of the lord of the field, but of an Israelite in whom there was no guile. He speaks out of the abundance of the faith of Israel. Ruth had nowhere hinted that she was showing kindness to her mother-in-law in leaving Moab for Israel, or that she was in the field to provide for her. How was it fully known to Boaz? He could have derived his knowledge only from narrations from Naomi herself, who in all likelihood had gratefully recounted her obligations to Ruth to the women of Bethlehem, unknown to her daughter-in-law. Ruth's faith in God and her love to her mother-in-law was noted and noticed and spoken about in the small village of Bethlehem. Of the Thessalonians later we read, *In every place your faith is spread abroad, so that we need not speak anything.... how ye turned to God from idols, to serve the living and true God* (1 Thesselonians 1:8,9).

71

Boaz was acquainted with Ruth's devotion to her husband's mother, showing great kindness to her after his death. Through Naomi she had been brought to trust the God of Israel and had left her father and mother and native land to accompany Naomi to Bethlehem, to accept the people of Israel as her people. It would seem that Abraham was in the mind of Boaz, who also was called by God and left his own country and his father's to go unto a land that God would show him (Genesis 12:1).

There seems also to be a further reference to Abraham in what follows: *The Lord recompense and a full reward be given thee.* God had said to Abraham, *I am thy exceeding great reward (Genesis 15:1).* As Ruth had done, as Abraham did — God would be her reward, as he was Abraham's.

THE PRAYER OF BOAZ FOR RUTH

The Lord recompense thy work, and a full reward be given thee of the Lord God of Israel, under whose wings thou art come to trust. (take refuge R.V.). (2:11,12)

These beautiful words of Boaz form one of the lesser known prayers of the Bible. He reverently owns Jehovah as the Lord, the God of Israel, and expresses his desire that He would recompense Ruth with peace (the word recompense is related to the word peace) and a full reward for her kindness to her mother-in-law. He is praying for the blessing of one who had found a covert and a shelter under Jehovah's wings. Ruth's trust was in the Lord. The beautiful expression "under Whose wings thou art come to take refuge" (R.V.) is a figure of speech derived from Deuteronomy 32:11; adopted by the Psalmist (Psalm 17:8, Psalm 36:7, Psalm 63:7, Psalm 91:1), and by Christ Himself (Matthew 23:37).

From this precious expression alone we could traverse a whole range of divine thought, presenting the glorious truth of the abiding place under the shadow of Jehovah's wings. The wings of God are first indicated from the traits of the eagle (Deuteronomy 32:11,12), and conclude with the traits of the hen (Matthew 23:37). The imagery of an eagle stirring up her nest, fluttering over her young, spreading abroad her wings, taking her young and bearing them on her pinions, is used as a picture of Jehovah's care and leading of His people. The final imagery of the hen spreading her wings to cover her young shows the safety under the shadow of the Almighty. The use of sheltering under her wings in the Psalms may be drawn from the shadow of the wings of the cherubim, whose wings spread over the holy place (Exodus 25:20). *He that dwelleth in the secret place of the most high shall abide under the shadow of the almighty.... He shall cover thee with His feathers, and under His wing shalt thou trust (Psalm 91:1,4).*

The knowledge of God's grace in the descriptive language used by Boaz in His prayer is a pattern of intelligence and thoughtfulness, to all who would draw near to the throne of grace. This short prayer was finally answered. God in an unusual way caused Boaz to be the divine means to answer his own petition.

And she said, let me find favour in thine eyes, my Lord; for that thou hast comforted me, and for that thou hast spoken to the heart of thine handmaid, though I be not like unto one of thine handmaids. (Ruth 2:13 R.V.)

The main form of diction used by the Holy Spirit in communicating the narrative, and fixing the events upon the mind of the reader, is dialogue. Fifty eight of the 85 verses in the book contain this primary device. In this beautiful chapter, there are more of these than in the rest of the book. It begins with Ruth and Naomi's conversation (verses 1, 2) and ends with the same (verses 19-23). This is the form of speech used for the words of Boaz to his reapers and their reply (verses 3,4); also between Boaz and his steward and his reply (verses 6,7). Then Boaz spoke to Ruth and she responded (verses 8,9,10). Boaz spoke again to Ruth and she responded (verses 11-14). Then Boaz spoke to his young men (verses 15,16). Finally, the voice of Boaz is heard speaking in prayer to Jehovah, the Lord God of Israel (verse 12).

Following the prayer of Boaz the heart of Ruth was comforted, *with good words even comfortable words*. Furthermore the phrase "spoken friendly" rightly means "spoken to the heart." Ruth was touched by his prayer to God for her, by his praise of her, and by his ministry which reached her heart. Ruth the "stranger" had her faith and hope in God strengthened. Many a handmaid would have been flattered and exalted by such an interest shown by the lord of the field; however, she showed a spirit of humility. Her desire was to be in the enjoyment of his continued favour, although she was not on equality with one of the lowest of his hired servant maids.

And Boaz said unto her at mealtime, Come thou hither, and eat of the bread, and dip thy morsel in the vinegar, and she sat beside the reapers, and he reached her parched corn, and she did eat and was supplied and left. (2:14)

The obedience of Ruth to the words of Boaz was one of the great secrets of the blessings which she enjoyed. The words of Mary are of value to young believers, *Whatsoever he saith unto you - do it (John 2:5)*. Whatever Boaz told Ruth to do, she quickly obeyed: and what was the result? An increasing knowledge of his person, and blessing on her service. The example for us is patent: We ought to do what he tells us, whatever it is. Boaz saw the great need of rest, refreshment and fellowship, following times of labour. Ruth *sat down under his shadow with great delight and his fruit was sweet to her taste,* and over the simple gathering was the banner of love. Ruth received a special portion from his own hand which satisfied her fully, and some she reserved, for those for whom nothing was prepared (Naomi).

And when she was risen up to glean. Boaz commanded his young men, saying, let her glean among the sheaves, and reproach her not: and let fall also some or the handfuls of purpose, and leave them, that she may glean them and forbid her not. So she gleaned in the field until even, and beat out what she had gleaned, and it was about an ephah of barley. (2:15-17)

Following the time of resting and refreshment, Ruth did not linger, but returned with resolve to continue in the tedious work of gleaning. Not only did Boaz command his workers to allow her a place to glean among the sheaves, but to let fall handfuls of purpose, so that she might have an abundant supply. This was an evidence of his personal generosity to the stranger going far beyond the requirements of the law. *And when ye read the harvest of your land, thou shalt not reap the corners of thy field, neither shalt thou gather the gleanings of thy harvest. Thou shalt leave them for the poor and the stranger; I am the Lord your God (Leviticus 19:9,10). When thou reapest thy field, and hast forgot a sheaf, thou shalt not go to fetch it, it shall be for the stranger, the fatherless and for the widow, that the Lord thy God may bless thee in all the works of thy hand (Deuteronomy 24:19).* Ruth is given a place in the field far beyond the limitations of the law of the harvest.

The term "handfuls of purpose" was a precious word to Ruth. She had truly found grace in the eyes of the lord of the harvest. Such an evidence of favour was a special feature of his field alone. She had received parched corn from the hand of Boaz, but these handfuls were dropped by his servants. All who minister the word should seek to minister to the special needs of the saints, especially dropping simple words with the purpose of feeding those newly come to the faith. There is a difference between Boaz reaching her parched corn and telling his servants to let handfuls of purpose fall for her. Did you ever experience a message given that seemed as though the servant could read your thoughts, or that someone had revealed to him your need? The word was exactly suited to your situation and state of mind. "Handfuls of purpose" are blessed when given by God. How they encourage the gleaner, increasing our fruits, blessing our efforts, multiplying results, and causing praise to ascend (verse 20).

The merciful character of Boaz regarding the poor and needy is a wonderful example to us to have compassion and an open hand to those who are hungry and homeless. *He that hath pity upon the poor lendeth unto the Lord, and that which he hath given will He pay again (Proverbs 19:17).*

"Handfuls of Purpose" or "Lending to the Lord"

That which we spend for others is well spent:
Men call it given, but God calls it lent,
We freely cast it, seed of His, to feed
The sparrows of His world, who most it need,
In fields and byways many a tiny grain,
Falls, and seems wasted, which shall spring again,
Into a full, ripe wheat sheaf by and by;
For life within the hard gold shell doth lie;
Life that can only pierce the husk and grow,
By being scattered where God's soft winds blow!

From "The Witness" 1932, J. H. Stuart

76

III. THE PROGRESS OF THE STRANGER

So she gleaned in the field until even, and beat out that which she had gleaned, and it was about an ephah of barley. And she took it up, and went into the city: and her mother-in-law saw what she had gleaned: and she brought forth, and gave to her that which she has reserved after she was sufficed. And her mother-in-law said unto her, Where hast thou gleaned today? and where wroughtest thou? blessed be he that did take knowledge of thee. And she shewed her mother-in-law with whom she had wrought, and said, the man's name with whom I wrought today is Boaz. And Naomi said unto her daughter-in-law, Blessed be he of the Lord, who hath not left of His kindness to the living and the dead. And Naomi said unto her, The man is near of kin unto us, one of our next of kinsmen. And Ruth the Moabitess said, He said unto me also, Thou shalt keep fast by my young men, until they have ended all my harvest. And Naomi said unto Ruth her daughter-in-law, It is good my daughter, that thou go out with his maidens, that they meet not in another field. So she kept fast by the maidens of Boaz to glean unto the end of barley harvest, and of wheat harvest; and dwelt with her. (2:17-23)

Boaz could have given her an ephah of barley, but he left her to stoop to gather, and glean and beat it out. Her labouring until even was the price she would pay for her barley. Boaz saw in Ruth features of a virtuous woman, as did all in Bethlehem. In the hard and wearisome task of gleaning, *she girded her loins with strength and made strong her arm (Proverbs 31:17)*. She commenced the day well, and ended it well, still gleaning. So may the saints and servants continue to glean and gather from the field of the Word of God, bread enough and to spare for the sustenance of spiritual life in their own soul, but also for those who require comfort. This should be the constant desire of our heart till the evening of life.

When Ruth ate her meal, Boaz saw that she kept a portion of it. When he saw her intention to share the remainder of the parched corn with Naomi, he gave the instructions to let sheaves fall to increase her gleaning. Few ever would have so much to show for a long day's toil in the hot sun. Ruth in the evening beat out about an ephah of barley. An ephah is commonly taken to be about 22 litres dry capacity and weighing around 15 kilograms. It appears that an ephah contained ten omers, and that one omer of manna was sufficient for one person's food for one day (Exodus 16:36). Therefore Ruth had gathered enough to keep her and Naomi five days.

She beat out what she had gleaned. The place of gathering was also a place of preparation to carry home the "beaten out" ears of barley. This was done with a rod, which freed the kernel from the chaff by beating, making it easier to carry home the pure barley. The spiritual lesson is evident: Gleaning in the scriptures must be followed by beating out in meditation. *The slothful man roasteth not that which he took in hunting (Proverbs 12:27).* He never enjoyed what he had taken by making it his own, and produced nothing for others. *But the substance of a diligent man is precious (Proverbs 12:27).* The Lord Jesus stated, *Every scribe which is instructed unto the kingdom of heaven is like unto a man that is an house-holder which bringeth forth out of his treasure things new and old (Matthew 13:52).* The ephah was a foretaste of future blessing, but of this Ruth had no knowledge as yet; however, she was thankful that her present need and the need of her mother-in-law had been fully supplied.

Her mother-in-law saw what she had gleaned (2:18). We are sure that Naomi waited, and kept watching for Ruth's return from her first day in the harvest field. With what joy the results of Ruth's toil was laid before Naomi, as she looked with wonder at the quantity. Ruth also gave her that portion of the corn which she had reserved for her from the mid-day meal. Unlike the widows who were neglected in the daily ministration in Jerusalem (Acts 6:1), Naomi knew the care of God in providing for her in meeting her daily need. *Where hast thou gleaned today? Where wroughtest thou?(2:19).* These personal questions are eminently practical to every child of God. Have we spent time gleaning in the wonderful pages of God's precious Word today? Where did you glean? Have we beaten out gathered sheaves on the threshing floor of heart meditation? In the case of Ruth, her profiting appeared to Naomi. *Meditate upon these things; give thyself wholly to them; that thy profiting may appear to all (1 Timothy 4:15).*

The answer to Naomi's question led to Ruth's first mention of his precious name, she had been with Boaz. The evidence of this was unmistakeable. The others who had wrought with Christ were taken knowledge of by many saying, *They have been with Jesus (Acts 4:13).* When Naomi heard that Ruth's benefactor was Boaz, she burst forth in a wonderful prayer of praise and thanksgiving, *Blessed be he of the Lord, who hath not left off his kindness to the living, and to the dead (Ruth 2:20).* What a change in attitude is expressed here by Naomi, compared with her previous view of God's dealings when she had first arrived in Bethlehem, *Call me not Naomi, call me Mara (bitterness), for the Almighty hath dealt very bitterly with me. I went out full, and the Lord hath brought me home again empty. Why then call ye me Naomi (pleasantness) seeing the Lord hath testified against me, and the Almighty hath afflicted me? (Ruth 1: 20,21).* On that occasion she complained bitterly at the trials and sorrows that were hers, not knowing the final purposes of the Lord, *That the Lord is very pitiful, and of tender mercy (James 5:11).* On that first day in Bethlehem she said, *The hand of the Lord is gone out against me.* But now on another first day she confesses, *The Lord hath not left off His kindness (hesed).*

The prayer of Naomi in which she used the word "blessed" presents the change in her spirit of bitterness to blessedness. Upon the mention of the name of the man with whom Ruth had become acquainted in the field, new hopes filled her heart. One of the most interesting words in her short ascription of praise is "kindness." Used three times in the Book of Ruth (chapter 1:8, 2:20, 3:10), it is one of the key words. The word is "hesed" (Hebrew) and is much richer in meaning than the English word. First it refers to the Lord Himself, who is a God of kindness. It involves divine grace in that His kindness is extended to the undeserving. David desired to shew kindness to Mephibosheth to fulfil his covenant with Jonathan (1 Samuel 20:42). In his generosity in giving Mephibosheth a place at his table as a king's son, David went far beyond what his covenant with Jonathan required, it was in fact *the kindness of God* (2 Samuel 9:3). Naomi expressed the kindness of God to be the source of her joy and hope, *The Lord hath not left off His kindness to the living and to the dead (chapter 2:20)*. There is a wonderful profession of faith in this prayer of Naomi in which she states her belief that her husband and two sons are in paradise and are still enjoying the kindness of God. How else could God's kindness be extended to them? The Lord Jesus later stated the same truth, *I am the God of Abraham, and the God of Isaac, and the God of Jacob. God is not the God of the dead but of the living (Matthew 22:32,33)*. The Sadducees could not answer, they could not grasp his teaching, yet 1300 years earlier Naomi understood that her loved ones were existing beyond death. To her God was indeed the God of the living.

The man is near of kin unto us, one of our next kinsman (chapter 2:20). Naomi suddenly recalled the relationship of Boaz, and exclaimed to Ruth "The man is near of kin to us" and then explained "He is one who is a go'el to us." The twenty occurrences of the verb "redeemed" in so short a book is a key to the wonderful subject of redemption. As well as the word "redeem" (Hebrew ga'al), the "redeemer" (Hebrew go'el) is repeated many times. The go'el translated "kinsman" is full of rich meaning. It conveys the right of one to redeem. The word is used in reference to our Lord Jesus: *I will help thee, saith the Lord and thy Redeemer (Isaiah 41:14).*

The law of the family life in Israel concerning redemption had two features which must be clearly understood, to appreciate the implications involved in the narrative of Ruth and Boaz in Ruth 3 and 4. The first is the 'go'el,' The second is the 'levir.'

These two family institutions require study so that a clear conception would enhance the generous and willing response of Boaz, who was the only redeemer who had the ability to meet all the claims of the law insomuch that he combined in himself the requirements of both 'go'el' and 'levir'. In this he foreshadows the Great 'Go'el' who would descend from Him.

1. The go'el: The duty of the kinsman (go'el) was to buy back the inheritance of a poor relation, who through poverty had been compelled to sell. *If thy brother hath waxen poor, and hath sold away of his possessions, and if any of his kin come to redeem it, then shall he redeem that which his brother hath sold (Leviticus 25:25).*

Also the persons themselves could be redeemed by the go'el. This duty is also revealed in Leviticus. *And if a sojourner or stranger was rich by thee, and thy brother dwelleth by thee wax poor, and sell himself unto the stranger or sojourner by thee, or to the stock of the stranger's family: after that he is sold he may be redeemed again. Any that is nigh of kin unto him of his family may redeem him; or if he be able he may redeem himself (Leviticus 25:47-49).*

Again the go'el had the God-given right to avenge a murder (Numbers 35:12).

2. The Levir: This word Levir means 'a husband's brother.' The levirate marriage practice is only mentioned in three passages in the scriptures of the Old Testament: Genesis and Deuteronomy 25:5-10 and Ruth. It is interesting that both are together referred to in this Book of Ruth alone. The first is the story of Judah and Er, his son's wife, Tamar. Er died without children, so levirate as a family

This Ruth

custom was necessary. The rest of the story is a sad one but shows the sense of duty to the dead brother's name to perpetuate his name through a son.

The law was not yet given in Genesis 38, but was added afterward. It is stated in Deuteronomy 25:5,6. _If brethren dwell together, and one of them die, and have no child, the wife of the dead shall not marry without unto a stranger: her husband's brother shall... take her to wife, and perform the duty of a husband's brother unto her. And it shall be that the firstborn which she beareth shall succeed in the name of his brother which is dead, that his name be not put out of Israel._

In this law of levirate marriage, a provision was made for any brother who did not wish to perform the responsibility of taking his dead brother's wife as his. There was a most humiliating sentence placed on the man who refused. _Then the elders of the city shall call him, and if he persists saying, I will not take her, then his brother's wife shall go up to him in the presence of the elders, and pull his sandal from his foot, and spit in his face; and she shall say, So shall it be done unto the man that will not build up his brother's house. And the name of his house shall be called in Israel, The house of him that hath the loosed shoe_ (Deuteronomy 25:8-10).

The Lord Jesus is foreshadowed in the 'go'el' and 'levir' in four beautiful ways: Kinsman, Redeemer, Bridegroom and Avenger.

1. **As the near Kinsman** we would consider His birth and incarnation: what He became, "God sent forth His Son; born of a woman, to redeem" (Galatians 4:4; John 1:14; Romans 1:3; Hebrews 2:14).

2. **As the Redeemer** we see His death, burial, and resurrection: what He accomplished. He paid the price of redemption (Ephesians 1:7, 1 Peter 1:18,19). He bought us with His own precious blood at the cross. Thank God we can say, "I know that my Redeemer liveth."

3. **As the Bridegroom:** What He will do. We look forward to

82

His coming again to receive us unto Himself (John 14:1,2). Here is the rapture of the Bride. *Christ loved the church and gave Himself for it (Ephesians 5-25).* He is coming to present the Bride unto Himself.

4. As the Avenger: What He will be to sinners. He will be the Avenger who will stand at the latter day upon the Mount of Olives.

In the Prophecy of Isaiah, one of the great key words is the Redeemer, which is used 24 times and covers the ideas of Kinsman, Redeemer and Avenger.

1. The Grace of the Kinsman: He is described as Immanuel (God with us). *For unto us a child is born, unto us a Son is given (Isaiah 9:6).* Here is the true Kinsman, His true humanity and His Eternal Sonship seen in one glorious Person as the One whose name is Wonderful.

2. The Greatness of the Redeemer: He is described as the Man of Sorrows, and presented in His redemptive work in Isaiah 53, the Redeemer paying the price of redemption.

3. The Glory of the Avenger: He who is presented in the opening of Isaiah as the Kinsman, in the central section as the Redeemer, is in the last part the Avenger, *I will tread them in mine anger... For the day of vengeance is in my heart... and the year of my Redeemed is come (Isaiah 63:3,4).* Israel's King will come back in judgment upon the ungodly of the world as the Messiah of the nation. We might add the beautiful words of Isaiah concerning the redeemed nation of Israel: *Thou also shall be a crown of glory in the hand of the Lord, and a royal diadem in the hand of thy God... and as the Bridegroom rejoiceth over the Bride, so shall thy God rejoice over thee (Isaiah 62:3,5).* The words of these verses can readily apply to the Bride of this age and certainly the rejoicing of the Bridegroom at His reception of the Bride.

So Naomi taught Ruth the glorious truth of the Kinsman Redeemer. Here we have a pattern of the words of Titus concerning the aged women, *The aged women... teachers of good (healthful) things, that they may teach the young women... to be discreet and chaste* (Titus 2:3-5).

The fact had dawned upon Naomi, based upon the kindness of God in him shown to Ruth, that he, the near kinsman, would take Ruth to be his bride. Ruth further told Naomi of the gracious welcome for her to remain in his field for the duration of the harvest, and that she was not to go to glean in another field. Naomi impressed this injunction upon Ruth, reminding her of the danger of other fields, where the high standard of purity of the field of Boaz was lacking. It was a warning of the low morale in those days of lawlessness which marked the times when the judges ruled.

To these words of her wise teacher Ruth gave heed. The closing verse in this remarkable chapter states, *So she kept fast by the maidens of Boaz to glean unto the end of barley harvest and wheat harvest, and dwelt with her mother-in-law* (Ruth 2:23).

It is of practical value to us to follow her example that they meet us not in any other save the field of our Redeemer, whether it be political, worldly pleasure, or religious, or in the companionship of any save His people. The barley harvest occurred during March and April, and the wheat harvest followed in June and July. Ruth was in the fields of Boaz keeping busy in His service, and providing for her needs and Naomi's. The experience of the first day when he spake to her heart was followed by many other meetings with him. From the story the impression is made that Boaz loved Ruth from the first sight of her as a stranger. When Jacob served seven years for Rachel, they seemed unto him but a few days, for the love he had to her. Glimpses of her beauty caused the waiting time to be as naught. So in the field, Boaz would see Ruth and Ruth would listen to his voice, both no doubt anticipating with joy the day of redemption (Ephesians 4:30).

The record of the first day was typical of all the days of the harvest. Ruth esteemed Boaz above all others, and he admired the evidences of a true virtuous woman (chapter 3:11). An understanding of this enhances the unusual aspects of Ruth at his feet in the next chapter.

And this I pray that your love may abound yet more and more (Philippians 1:9).

More and More

More coming out from all that hinders me,
More separation, O my Lord, to Thee —
Self crucified, and all that self involves;
More trust in Thee and less of high resolves,
More patient prayer, more Bible, and more love;
Eyes less on earth and more on God above;
A life that deepens in the things of God,
Enduring hardness, bowing to the rod;
Christ all my hope, and not from Him apart,
Himself my Pilot and His Word my chart —
So shall I weather life's tempestuous sea,
And find eternal peace, my Lord with Thee.

C. Butler Stoney

The Rest of the Way

O fathomless mercy, O infinite grace
In humble thanksgiving, the road I retrace
Thou never hast failed me, my strength and my stay:
To whom should I turn for the rest of the way?

Through danger, through darkness, by day and by night

Thou ever has guided and guided aright
I have trusted in Thee and peacefully lay
My head in Thy hand for the rest of the way.

Thy cross all my refuge, Thy blood all my plea
None other I need, blest Redeemer, but Thee
I fear not the shadows at the close of life's day
For Thou wilt go with me the rest of the way.

Laura Kern Sawyer

The Plan of God

3

This sacred chapter requires the help of the gracious Person of the Holy Spirit to understand the many spiritual lessons, as the narrative reaches the turning point. It is the beginning of the lifting of Ruth out of obscurity into a happy union with Boaz, the mighty man of wealth. The first recorded history of a rise from rags to riches, from penury to plenty, from tears to triumph, from Moabitish worship to Messianic witness, advances to the ultimate in the scenes of the threshing floor. It is much more than the account of an alien and one of the chosen race being brought into relationship, but a blessed foreshadowing of the divine union between Christ and all who trust in Him and are His by grace.

In contrast to the field, where with others Ruth shared fellowship, food, and the ministry of the redeemer, we are now introduced to her personal communion with him. In chapter two, Boaz approaches her; in this chapter Ruth seeks him. Ruth had been fed by his hand; she now seeks rest at his feet. In the field many blessings were enjoyed, now she desires to be with the blesser himself. In the previous chapter Ruth found shelter under the wings of Jehovah, here she desires Boaz to shelter her with his skirt (wing).

The three important sections of this wonderful chapter of Ruth are full of grace and truth: I. **The Present Ministry of the Redeemer** (verses 1,2); II. **The Preparation for the Presence of the Redeemer** (verses 3-7); III. **The Promised Prospect of Redemption** (verses 8-18).

I. THE PRESENT MINISTRY OF THE REDEEMER

Then Naomi her mother-in-law said unto her, my daughter, shall I not seek rest for thee, that it might be well with thee? And now is not Boaz of our kindred, with whose maidens thou wast? Behold he winnoweth barley tonight in the threshing floor. (3:1,2)

The consideration of Naomi and Ruth for one another is an example. When daily provision was needed Ruth laboured in the field on behalf of Naomi, but now Naomi has a plan to bring happiness for Ruth. The question of Naomi expresses her heart's desire for Ruth, *My daughter, shall I not seek rest for thee, that it may be well with thee? (Ruth 3:1).* This question echoes her prayer on the Bethlehem road, when she asked God to give her daughters-in-law rest with another husband. On that occasion she was unable to give what she desired for Ruth, but now she sees a glorious possibility. It was a dark day then, but now she sees sunshine through the clouds. The 'rest' which Naomi sought was to be settled securely in a home with a suitable husband. We must also take into account that it was the custom for Hebrew parents to arrange marriages for their children (Genesis 24:1-5). Any bride expected in a home provided by her husband she would find rest and care for her lifetime with protection and provision, and above all, love.

This is a rest that, alas, is lacking in many marriage unions today. It should be the aim of every husband to bestow such a home of rest and love (Ephesians 5:25). This blessed union is a beautiful figure of the union of Christ and His Church. It also pictures personal relationship with Him, bringing rest in this life, and the prospect of eternal rest in our home above (Matthew 11:28, Hebrews 4:9). As a bride leans in dependence and fully trusts her husband, so does the bride of Christ trust and depend on her beloved Lord and Bridegroom (Song of Solomon 8:5). In the directions given to her daughter-in-law to go personally into the presence of Boaz, Naomi manifested an unselfish spirit of grace by seeking favour for Ruth the Moabitess rather than for herself, the wife of his late kinsman. Naomi was in the same spirit as one of God's greatest servants who hundreds of years later wrote of his desire for his children in the faith, *I do not seek yours but you; for the children ought not to lay up for the parents, but the parents for the children. Now I shall most gladly spend and be spent for your souls (2 Corinthians 12:14,15)*.

Both the examples of unselfish love, in Naomi and Paul, call for our spiritual emulation. No doubt having considered the law of God carefully with regard to the 'go'el' and the 'levir', Naomi now proceeds to prepare Ruth to immediately make that claim upon Boaz, which was her right. Naomi had sufficient insight by the reports from Ruth that Boaz would be favourable and become Ruth's redeemer and bridegroom.

In order to come into his presence there must be a knowledge of his person and the place where he is found. Naomi instructed Ruth and identified his person, *Is not Boaz of our kindred?* He is therefore the person to whom the Word of God directs as the redeemer. The question of Job could have now been in Ruth's heart; *Oh that I knew where I might find Him, that I might come even to His seat (Job 23:3)*. Naomi knew not only His person but where to find him, *Behold, he winnoweth barley tonight in the threshingfloor (verse 2)*.

The threshingfloors of the Bible have significant lessons:

1. The threshingfloor of Ornan (1 Chronicles 21:18-27). At this place an altar was built by David at great cost and he offered burnt offerings and peace offerings and called upon the Lord. The cause was great, for over Jerusalem was a drawn sword. But God commanded the sword to be sheathed. He had accepted the sacrifice. This first threshingfloor has its answer at Calvary. It speaks of the death and resurrection of the Lord.

2. The threshingfloor of Gideon (Judges 6:36-40). The fleece of Gideon upon the threshingfloor of Gideon was wet with the dew of heaven while the earth was dry. This speaks in type of the descent of the Holy Spirit.

3. The threshingfloor of Christ (Matthew 3:12). He, when He returns, shall thoroughly purge His threshingfloor, and burn up the chaff with unquenchable fire. Here we have the return of the Lord in judgment.

4. The threshingfloor of Boaz (Ruth 3:2). The Lord of the harvest is winnowing barley today. He is coming as Judge of all the earth on another day to gather the wheat into His barn and to burn the chaff with unquenchable fire. Today He removes the husk from the grain. This winnowing the harvest is a picture of The Present Ministry of Christ.

Ruth was to come to Boaz as the one who winnowed, one who would rid himself of all chaff. What is morally worthless can have no place with him. One has said, "It is better to be winnowed by Christ, than sifted by Satan." Christ winnows to get rid of the chaff but Satan sifts to destroy the wheat, if it were possible. Ruth represents one who had such preparations for his presence that there was no chaff, she was morally accepted in his sight. We shall therefore consider the second section where her preparation was completed.

The Book of Ruth is exquisite in merit from a literary standpoint. The story moves smoothly from the sadness of Moab to the gladness of Bethlehem. Chapter one is a demonstration of faith seen in the resolve of Ruth making her wonderful choice. Following in the next chapter we see her devotion of hope in seeking to appropriate the resources of grace. In this spiritual third chapter is her desire of love, thus she made request to claim her rights to union with the redeemer. It could be said that in these opening parts of the book, Ruth leaves a spiritual record: How to turn to God; how to grow in grace; how to approach the Lord. This is a pattern for young Christians today. It is an illustration of genuine allegiance to the Lord, of growth through activity in gleaning from the scriptures, and of getting into the presence of God with reverence of approach.

II. THE PREPARATION FOR THE PRESENCE OF THE REDEEMER

Wash thyself therefore, and anoint thee, and put thy raiment unto thee, and get thee down to the floor: But make not thyself known to the man, until he shall have done eating and drinking. And it shall be, when he lieth down, that thou shalt mark the place where he shall lie, and thou shalt go in, and uncover his feet, and lay thee down; and he will tell thee what thou shalt do. And she said unto her, all that thou sayest unto me I will do. And she went down unto the floor, and did all that her mother-in-law bade her. And when Boaz had eaten and drunk, and his heart was merry, he went to lie down at the end of the heap of corn; and she came softly and uncovered his feet, and laid her down. (3:3-7)

The three things that were necessary before Ruth could take her place at the feet of Boaz have a clear application to all believers who would seek to approach to God. Some may think that the plan of Naomi for Ruth was unconventional, immodest, and indiscreet, and that the claim could have been a different time and place. But against this we see her confidence in God to carry out the instructions of the word of God. Naomi acted as a "mother in Israel." Ruth was a virtuous woman, and Boaz a man of absolute integrity.

Ruth must first be washed to meet her lord. She must wash herself. There must be no stain upon her when she meets Boaz. This washing means purity. With regard to Israel, there were many ceremonial washings before entrance into the worship of Jehovah. To enjoy the place of nearness to the Lord we must be *cleansed from all filthiness of the flesh and spirit, perfecting holiness in the sight of God* (2 Corinthians 7:1). The divine command of God is, *Wash you, make you clean, put away the evil of your doings from before mine eye* (Isaiah 1:16). The answer of an exercised heart is, *Purge me with hyssop and I shall be clean, wash me, and I shall be whiter than snow* (Psalm 51:7). To be in the presence of God we must present ourselves in purity, otherwise worship is formal and the power of God cannot be known. Our blessed Lord in the upper room took a towel and a basin filled with water to wash His disciples' feet. He said that they could have no part with Him unless their feet were washed (John 13:8).

The second thing Ruth must do was to anoint herself (Ruth 3:3). She was to pour fragrant oil upon her person. The gracious Holy Spirit is the anointing today. Every born again person has received this anointing (1 John 2:20-27). The importance of the fragrance of the working of the Holy Spirit in our lives is vital to the enjoyment of nearness to God. There can be no fellowship at His feet apart from the Person of the Holy Spirit (Ephesians 1:13-14, 4:30-32).

Third, Ruth must lay aside the garments of widowhood and put on garments suited for his presence. In the place of sadness, joy now marks her, as she makes ready her "best attire" for him. Finally the Bride of the Lamb will be presented to Christ adorned in raiment pure and white (Revelation 19:8, 21:2). The believer is to put on the Lord Jesus Christ (Romans 13:14), and *as the elect of God kindness, humbleness of mind and meekness (Colossians 3:12)*. These features of spiritual value were all evident in Ruth in her approach to her redeemer.

Further instructions were given by Naomi that when she would go to the threshing floor, she was not to reveal herself to him until he had finished eating and drinking. Having prepared herself for his presence, Ruth must learn how to present herself to him. Ruth washed, anointed, and robed represents suitability for the presence of the Lord. *Let us draw near with a true heart, in full assurance of faith, having our hearts sprinkled from an evil conscience, and our bodies washed with pure water (Hebrews 10:22)*. All who come to God in such a way, He will shew them what to do, and will complete the matter this day on their behalf, as Boaz did for Ruth.

We learn of the availability of spiritual blessings in Christ, but as Ruth we must take the initiative in seeking Him and His resources. The Lord would encourage this through His words, *They that seek me early shall find me, riches and honour are with me, yea durable riches and righteousness. My fruit is better than gold, and my revenue than choice silver: I lead in the way of righteousness, in the midst of the paths of judgment; that I may cause those that love me to inherit substance; and I will fill their treasuries (Proverbs 8:17-21 R.V.)*. Humility, submission, and modesty were all seen in Ruth. These beautiful moral qualities, however, were not sufficient to gain the wealth of Boaz or union with his person. She must move towards him in the attitude of need, as one who desired his protection, compassion and love.

A further direction given by Naomi is worthy of spiritual consideration: *And it shall be, when he lieth down, that thou shalt mark the place where he shall lie, and thou shalt go in, and uncover his feet, and lay thee down; and he will tell thee what thou shalt do (Ruth 3:4)*. *Mark the place where he shall lie.* Every believer should mark places where the Saviour lay and seek to identify with the grace of our Lord Jesus Christ.

1. **Lying in a manger** (Luke 2:12) - **His lowliness.** We behold the greatness of His stoop; *He became poor* (2 *Corinthians* 8:9). Consider: the marvel, majesty, meaning, mercy and message of the manger. "Lying in a manger" shows the extent of His poverty, the attitude of the world, the availability of His Person, the devotion of the Servant, but to the believer it is the example of humility. Writing to the saints at Philippi, during a time of personal difference among sisters, Paul presents Christ in the lowliness of His pathway of humility as the pattern for His followers, *Let this mind be in you, which was also in Christ Jesus... who was found in fashion as a man (Philippians 2:5-8).* No one can mark His place of humiliation in the manger without bearing likeness to His grace.

2. **Lying on a pillow** (Mark 4:38) – **His grace.** We behold the wonder of His humanity. The Lord asleep on the steersman's pillow, was truly a perfect Man, but He was also truly God, who being awakened by the distressful cries of His disciples, arose and hushed the stormy gale and calmed the raging sea. He was the Son of God in possession of all power. The calming of the sea was a divine act, ascribed to Jehovah alone, *Jehovah, God of hosts, who is like unto Thee, the strong Jah. Thou rulest the pride of the Sea, when its waves arise, Thou stillest them* (Psalm 89:8,9; Psalm 107:23-32 *J.N.D.*). They said to one another, *What manner of man is this, that even the wind and the sea obey Him?* He was the Great Creator, creation had heard the Creator's voice, yet how slow the minds of men to realize the significance of His actions. The Jehovah of the Old Testament is the One who lies asleep on a pillow - what amazing grace!

3. **Lying in a Garden** (Matthew 26:39) - **His submission.** We behold the mystery of Gethsemane. The sinless Saviour was soon to become the Bearer of sin. This was the cause of His sorrow in the garden. He was looking ahead to that hour of deepest woe on Cal-

vary. In Luke's account, the Lord "kneeled" to pray, but in Matthew, He "fell on His face." Lying on His own earth was the King of Glory. His submission to His Father's will produced the deepest prayer from the lowest position.

Lepers had fallen on their faces before Him. One asked for cleansing (Luke 5:12), and one fell on his face to give Him thanks (Luke 17:16). Three disciples fell on their faces in the holy mount Matthew 17:6). One day, the elders in Heaven will fall on their faces to worship God (Revelation 11:16). None of these that fell on their faces ever knew the severe experience of the Lord as He fell on His face in complete submission to His Father's will. He was to drink the cup of judgment on the cross. What supreme devotion!

4. **Lying in a tomb** (Matthew 28:6), *Come see the place where the Lord lay.* – **His victory.** We behold the triumph of the Lord. The angel calmed the fears of the women at the tomb, and supplied them with wonderful information. The One whom they sought, Jesus of Nazareth, who had been crucified, was not in the garden tomb, He was risen. His glorious work was completed; the mighty triumph had been won, and He had conquered death and the grave.

The angelic words were true, *He is risen, He is not here, behold the place where they laid Him* (Mark 16:5-8). On entering the tomb, they found it empty. The linen clothes lay in their original windings, but they found not the body of the Lord Jesus. This wondrous triumph, announced by angels, witnessed by the empty tomb, and confirmed by the personal appearances of the Lord Himself, is the glorious proof of His bodily resurrection. The place where He lay has been exchanged for the place where He sits, at God's right hand in Heaven (Hebrews 1:3).

As we mark these places where He lay, our hearts overflow in worship and we sing from our hearts, "Hallelujah! What a Saviour!"

Ruth agreed to follow the instructions of her mother-in-law, saying, *All that thou sayest, I will do (Ruth 3:5).* What an example to young believers to be obedient to teaching ministry and to be consecrated to God. Ruth was not only a hearer of the word, but a doer of it. This carries the sure promise of blessing in the doing (James 1:22-25).

So Ruth came to the threshing floor and waited for the moment when Boaz would lie down. *When Boaz had eaten and drunken, and his heart was merry, and he went to lie down at the head of the heap of corn (Ruth 3:7).* Why was he merry? At the end of the day he ate and drank with a merry heart because of the joy of the harvest (Isaiah 9:3). God had abundantly blessed him. Being merry here has no thought of any excess of wine. It rather means that he was happy and contented.

In the east, threshing floors are situated close to the harvest fields. When the grain was threshed, the winnowing was done by throwing the grain up into the wind. This usually was in the evening. The chaff was blown away and the pure grain fell on the floor and was headed up at the end of the threshing floor. It was usual for the owner and his servants to sleep beside the harvest of grain, in order to guard their crops from thieves in the night. Men lay down in their clothes with a mantle over their feet for extra covering and warmth in the cold of the night.

When Boaz had laid down and was asleep, Ruth came softly and uncovered his feet and lay down. In the harvest field she bowed at his feet in response to his words, which reached her heart (Ruth 2:10). Four times in the threshing floor, his feet are mentioned. On this occasion, she is there to speak words to his heart that he might become her redeemer.

III. THE PROMISED PROSPECT OF REDEMPTION

And it came to pass at midnight, that the man was afraid, and

turned himself: and, behold, a woman lay at his feet. And he said, Who art thou? And she answered, I am Ruth thine handmaid: spread therefore thy skirt over thine handmaid; for thou art a near kinsman. And he said, Blessed be thou of the LORD, my daughter: for thou hast shewed more kindness in the latter end than at the beginning, inasmuch as thou followedst not young men, whether poor or rich. And now, my daughter, fear not; I will do to thee all that thou requirest: for all the city of my people doth know that thou art a virtuous woman. And now it is true that I am thy near kinsman: howbeit there is a kinsman nearer than I. Tarry this night, and it shall be in the morning, that if he will perform unto thee the part of a kinsman, well; let him do the kinsman's part: but if he will not do the part of a kinsman to thee, then will I do the part of a kinsman to thee, as the LORD liveth: lie down until the morning. (3:8-13)

One of the words in the Book of Ruth that indicates the main theme of the book is the word, "redemption." There are twenty-three mentions of the word ga'al in the Book of Ruth.

Boaz slept and Ruth, guided by God, came and lay at his feet. In the garden Adam slept, and God took a rib from his side and builded a woman, and brought her to the man. When Adam was awakened the woman was presented to him by the Lord as a suitable partner, companion and bride. Contrary to human ideas, it seems God's way to bring the woman to the man. Eve was brought to Adam, Rebekah to Isaac, Rachel to Jacob, Asenath to Joseph, and Abigail to David. When Boaz awakened and turned himself, he found a woman at his feet. When he asked her who she was, she replied: *I am Ruth thine handmaid.*

The name Ruth appears twelve times in this little book and once in the New Testament (Matthew 1:5). Her name is linked five times with Moab: Ruth the Moabitess (Ruth 1:22; 2:2,21; 4:5,10). It is linked with Boaz three times (Ruth 3:9, 4:10,13); with Naomi twice (Ruth 1:14, 2:22); with Mahlon once (Ruth 1:4); with God once (Ruth 1:16,17), and it is linked with Christ once (Matthew 1:5). In all the mentions of her name, she has fragrance, for *A good name is better than precious ointment* (Ecclesiastes 7:1).

Ruth, having identified herself as "Ruth thine handmaid" asked Boaz to spread his skirt over her; for he was the redeemer. Ruth was placing her claim, she was seeking his protection. Ruth knew he had power to redeem, and she had a right to apply to him as her near kinsman.

The words of Ruth are beautiful and significant, *Spread thy skirt over thine handmaid* (Ruth 3:9). The language is figurative and full of meaning. In one passage (Ezekiel 16:8), God speaks of His relationship with Israel under the figure of a marriage and said, *Now when I passed by thee, and looked upon thee, behold thy time was the time of love: and I spread my skirt over thee.*

It is interesting that the word "skirt" also means "wing". It recalls the harvest field; Boaz had used the same metaphor in speaking to the heart of Ruth, the gleaner, *The Lord recompense thy work, and a full reward be given thee of the Lord God of Israel, under whose wings thou art come to trust* (Ruth 2:12). It is not unlikely that Ruth had those gracious words of promise before her mind, as she lay at his feet, and so she said tenderly to Boaz, *Spread thy wing over thine handmaid.* When Ruth learned that the one who had been so gracious to her in his harvest field was her near kinsman, with the power to redeem, she was encouraged to place herself as one who needed his protection. The words of Ruth expressed, we believe, the faith of her heart that the "wing" of Boaz was one of the manifestations of the unseen "wings" of Jehovah.

Boaz realized the implications of the humble plea of the destitute widow at his feet. He considered that the God of Israel had led her from the darkness of Chemosh to the light of Jehovah. Her choice was known to him. He had seen her moral beauty and faithful service in the field of Bethlehem. Now she lay at his feet desiring his compassion and companionship, and he said, *Blessed be thou of the Lord my daughter, for thou has shown more kindness in the latter end than at the beginning, inasmuch as thou followedst not young men whether poor or rich (Ruth 3:10).*

This is the second recorded prayer of Boaz for God's blessing upon Ruth (Ruth 2:12). He deeply appreciated her last kindness (hesed) seen in not choosing young men, but placing her commitment to the family of Elimelech, by choosing him as the only way of redeeming the inheritance which was to be sold, and perpetuating the family name by raising up the name of the dead upon his inheritance. This is the meaning of Hesed, the word is used of God in 1:8 and 2:20. But here it is used of Ruth and is described as this last kindness to her new family relationship and to him as their near kinsman.

And now, my daughter, fear not, I will do to thee all that thou requirest. For all the city doth know that thou art a virtuous woman. (3:11)

The gracious commendation of Boaz complies with the description of the virtuous woman of Proverbs 31:10-31. Ruth was truly a virtuous woman; her price was "far above rubies." She worked willingly with her hands; she brought food for others, she girded her loins with strength, she stretched out her hand to the poor and needy, strength and honor were her clothing, in her tongue was the law of kindness, a woman that feared the Lord, thus earning praise; in the city gates her own works praised her. Following her marriage, the heart of her husband safely trusted in her, she did him good and not evil all the days of her life. Her husband was known in the gates, when he sat among the elders of the land.

It can be said also of Ruth, "Many daughters have done virtuously, but thou excellest them all." This full length spiritual portrait of a virtuous woman cannot be shown anywhere among all the women of scripture so fully as in the picture of Ruth. Not only did all the city of Bethlehem have this knowledge, but her virtue is spoken of in all the world, even to this day.

Since ancient Bible times, her name has ever been most popular among girls. Although there is only one Ruth in the Bible, Elsdon C. Smith in his excellent compilation of the first hundred names in North America, places Ruth seventh in the list, with an estimated number of almost one and a half million bearing the name. This use of her name honours her virtue and is a testimony to her godliness. *Favour is deceitful, and beauty is vain, but a woman that feareth the Lord she shall be praised (Proverbs 31:30).*

Boaz calmed the fears of Ruth with the tender words, "Fear not." This assuring expression was used by God to many, beginning with Abraham and ending with John (Genesis 15:1, Revelation 1:17). Boaz calmed her present fears and gave her the promise of a peaceful future. Our blessed Redeemer ministers the same to anxious hearts today. The pledge of the word of Boaz must have brought joy to Ruth, *I will do all to thee that thou requirest (Ruth 3:11).*

In this chapter we have considered Naomi's plan and Ruth's preparation; we now face Boaz's problem.

And now it is true that I am thy near kinsman, howbeit there is a kinsman nearer than I. Tarry this night, and it shall be in the morning, that if he will perform unto thee the part of a kinsman well, but if he will not do the part of a kinsman to thee, then will I do the part of a kinsman to thee; as the Lord liveth: lie down until the morning. (3:12,13)

The problem confronting Boaz was unknown to Ruth. A great

difficulty stood in the way of Boaz's response to the claim to do the part of a kinsman. There was a nearer kinsman than Boaz, who had the first right to redeem; until he accepted or refused to perform the part of a kinsman, Boaz could do nothing. The great concern of Boaz was the redemption of Ruth. Boaz made a promise that in the morning he would confer with the other kinsman and if he performed his part, well, but if not Boaz would be the go'el. This he pledged to Ruth by a vow, which revealed his desire to be her kinsman-redeemer and bridegroom. The confirmation of his promise by an oath, "As the Lord liveth" was the most solemn and binding any Hebrew could take on himself. Having received the promise of redemption Boaz requested her to lie down until the morning at his feet. It is evident that he meant to spread his wing of protection over Ruth, and perform for her whatever the law and his kindness might desire.

So she lay at his feet until the morning: and she rose up before one could know another, and he said, Let it not be known that a woman came into the floor. Also he said, bring the vail that thou hast upon thee and hold it, and when she held it, he measured six measures of barley, and laid it on her; and she went into the city. (3:14,15)

Before daybreak, and before others were stirring, Boaz sent Ruth away. His purpose was lest it be known that she had spent the night there. Boaz sought to preserve the good name of Ruth, and his own fidelity, from the insinuations of the gossips of Bethlehem, who would place a wrong interpretation on their meeting. Ruth, therefore departed early, so there would be no occasion for the adversary to speak reproachfully (1 Timothy 5:14). Some modern commentators, to our surprise, do suggest otherwise, seeking to damage the reputation of Ruth and Boaz. Perhaps they have damaged their own reputation by a poor understanding of the background and the context of the incident. The Holy Spirit teaches the honour and purity of Boaz and Ruth.

During her labors in the harvest field, she had received of the generosity of Boaz and had gleaned and beaten out enough food for a few days for herself and Naomi. But as a result of personal communion with Boaz, he poured six measures of barley into her vail (cloak), and laid it upon her head, the usual means of carrying such a burden. Thus Boaz crowned her with a mark of the lovingkindness of God (Psalm 103:4).

And when she came to her mother-in-law, she said, Who art thou my daughter? And she told her all the man had done to her. (3:16)

The question implies, "Are you the same as when you left to meet him? Are you still the widow of Mahlon or are you the betrothed of Boaz?" Naomi was anxious to hear all the facts of the meeting in the threshing floor, and how Boaz had specially designed that she would not return empty to her. This word empty was used by Naomi to describe her condition when she returned from Moab (Ruth 1:21). Now those empty days are about to conclude. It is interesting to notice that the last recorded words of Ruth are the message of Boaz, *Go not empty unto thy mother-in-law* (Ruth 3:17).

Then said she, sit still my daughter, until thou know how the matter will fall, for the man will not be in rest until he hath finished the thing this day. (3:18)

Naomi gave encouragement to Ruth, she had faith in Jehovah, and confidence in Boaz, that he would not rest until the work which he had begun would be completed. She must rest, sit still, and commit her way unto the Lord. It is difficult to wait, but the words of

Isaiah 30:7 state, *Their strength is to sit still.*

The words of Paul writing to the saints at Philippi seem to echo the words of Naomi, *He which hath begun a good work in you will perform it until the day of Jesus Christ (Philippians 1:6).* Boaz is presented as the tireless servant, the man who will not rest till the work of redemption is completed, which is the illustration of Christ as He is presented in Mark's Gospel. The delay for the completion of our redemption is also brief, *The man will not be in rest until he have finished the thing this day.*

These words can be applied to the love of our Lord Jesus Christ for His saints. While in this world He had no resting place until He accomplished our redemption, by the shedding of His precious blood. This was the redemption of our souls by the laying down of His life. Now He who loved us is at God's right hand exalted, but His love will not rest until the final phase of our redemption is consummated, the redemption of our bodies by His coming again. He longs for that moment and looks for that appointed time. Can we say "Even so come Lord Jesus?" (Revelation 22:20).

Yet it must be, Thy love had not its rest
were Thy Redeemed not with thee fully blest
That love that gives not as the world, but shares
All it possesses with its loved co-heirs.

The heart is satisfied can ask no more;
All thought of self is now forever o'er,
Christ, its unmingled object, fills the heart
In blest adoring love - its endless part.

John Nelson Darby

107

The True Messiah

Hail to the Lord's Anointed,
Great David's greater Son!
Hail, in the time appointed,
His reign on earth begun!
He comes to break oppression,
To set the captive free,
To take away transgression,
And rule in equity.

He shall come down like showers
Upon the fruitful earth;
Love, joy and hope like flowers,
Spring in His path to birth.
Before Him, on the mountains,
Shall peace, the herald, go;
And righteousness in fountains,
From hill to valley flow.

Arabia's desert-ranger
To Him shall bow the knee;
The Ethiopian stranger
His glory come to see;
With offerings of devotion
Ships from the isles shall meet,
To pour the wealth of oceans
In tribute at His feet.

Kings shall fall down before Him,
And gold and incense bring;

All nations shall adore Him,
His praise all people sing:
For He shall have dominion
O'er river, sea and shore
Far as the eagle's pinion,
Or dove's light wing, can soar.

For Him shall prayer unceasing
And daily vows ascend;
His kingdom still increasing -
A kingdom without end.
The mountain dew shall nourish
A seed in weakness sown,
Whose fruit shall spread and flourish,
And shake like Lebanon.

O'er every foe victorious,
He on His throne shall rest;
From age to age more glorious,
All blessing and all blest.
The tide of time shall never
His covenant remove;
His name shall stand forever,
His great, blest Name of Love.

James Montgomery

Faith's Reckonings

Back to the cross I look and wondering see
The Christ of God, dying instead of me;
But gazing closer at that form Divine
I see with Him - myself; His death was mine.

Again beside the garden tomb I stand,
And watch Him buried there with reverent hand;
But in that grave faith sees not one, but two,
God hid me there forever from His view.

But was that precious "Corn of Wheat" thus sown
In tears wasted, or did it rise alone?
A fruitful ear, bursting from 'neath the sod,
It rose in every grain, a saint of God.

Since then by simple faith ourselves we see,
Whether for death or life in Christ to be;
May the world henceforth in our words and ways
See Christ in us, to His continual praise.

Wm. Hoste

The Program
of God

4

The Book of Ruth begins with burial, but ends with birth. It commences with famine and tears, and ends with fame and triumph. The closing portion of the book could be called: "When God writes the closing chapter." This chapter provides practical lessons on the great value of living for God, as to the final profit and reward. But beside all this, the closing verses are evidence of the great prophetic program of God in the chosen list of names from Pherez to David, indicating the kingly line in which Christ the Messiah was to be born. Therefore the main purpose of the little Book of Ruth is disclosed (Ruth 4:18-22; Matthew 1:1-17). There are three sections to be considered: I. **The Supremacy of the Redeemer** (verses 1-12); II. **The Satisfaction of the Redeemed** (verses 13-17); III. **The Selection of the Redemptive Line** (verses 18-22).

I. THE SUPREMACY OF THE REDEEMER

Then went Boaz up to the gate, and sat him down there: and behold, the kinsman of whom Boaz spake came by: unto whom he

said, "Ha such a one! Turn aside sit down here, and he turned aside and sat down. And he took ten men of the elders of the city, and said, sit ye down here. And they sat down. (4:1,2)

God's word states plainly, *Better is the end of a thing than the beginning (Ecclesiastes 7:8)*. It could be rightly applied to this Book of Ruth. It is a remarkable fact that the end of the book is least known. The first two chapters are well-known, but the last two are less known. How this exquisite story ends is of great spiritual value.

It is interesting to observe that chapters 1 to 3 show Ruth's private life, whereas chapter 4 shows her public life. The spirit of God has chosen to inform us of her private and personal career in the opening chapter, but as is usual, the fourth in any series in scripture is a marked change from what precedes. Therefore, what is presented in the last chapter is a public display.

Chapter one: The decision expressed on the highway was her personal choice. Chapter two: The diligence revealed in the harvest field was her personal exercise. Chapter three: The devotional plea on the threshing floor was a personal matter. Chapter four: The destiny decided in the gate of the city was a public scene.

All the elders, all those who passed by, and the whole city had knowledge of her exaltation and of the redeemer's love towards her. Boaz owned her as his own.

What a lesson there is here for all saints: Our private choices to serve God, our diligence in His field, and our devotion to Christ, while unknown now, will one day be made public, when standing in His presence at the Judgment Seat of Christ (2 Corinthians 5:9,10). Ruth exchanges the garments of widowhood for bridal array. So of the Bride of Christ: *And to her was granted that she should be arrayed in fine linen, clean and white, for the fine linen is the righteousness of the saints (Revelation 19:8)*. In this chapter also we admire the supremacy of Boaz; in the earlier chapter, Ruth was the

116

chief subject, but not in chapter four. Boaz is the preeminent one. Authority and redeeming grace mark him. His name is famous in Israel. Ruth's destiny is linked with him who bears the glory, in his sufficiency to redeem the land and his bride, to the satisfaction of God's law.

BOAZ WENT UP TO THE GATE.

The open space at the gate, was the place where local decisions were made by the elders and business transactions settled. The gate of Bethlehem had already witnessed a great part of the story. Elimelech with his family had passed through its portals in their path of departure to Moab. Naomi and Ruth entered years later: poor, friendless and desolate. It had seen Ruth going forth to the harvest field every morning, and returning with her hard earned gleanings every evening. It was but fitting that at the same gate the glorious ending should be enacted.

Boaz is a wonderful type of Christ. He was the redeemer. The key to this chapter is redemption, by paying the price, "redeem" is used seven times, "redeeming," once, "redeemer," four times, and "buy" five times. The blessed Person of Christ is titled "Redeemer" at least sixteen times in the Old Testament, but never in the New Testament, yet His redeeming work proclaims Him the Great Redeemer. Whenever the truth is presented it means to set free by paying a price. Boaz in the gate foreshadows the Lord Jesus in two ways: It was there He laid the foundation of redemption. It was a public place, "This thing was not done in a corner." He also foreshadows Christ in exaltation, in His risen power, sitting on the right hand of God. *The mighty man of wealth (1 Peter 1:11).*

In the gate where Boaz was seated, the nearer kinsman came by and Boaz asked him to sit down. Boaz also invited the elders to join and witness the transaction. The gates usually had a place where twelve men could be seated, and many spectators would assemble, standing to hear the proceedings.

And he said unto the kinsman, Naomi, that is come again out of the country of Moab, selleth a parcel of land, which was our brother Elimelech's. And I thought to disclose it to thee, saying buy it before the inhabitants, and before the elders of my people. For thou wilt redeem it, but if thou wilt redeem it tell me, that I may know, for there is none to redeem it beside thee and I am after thee. And he said, I will redeem it. Then said Boaz, What day thou buyest the field of the hand of Naomi, thou must buy it also of Ruth the Moabitess, the wife of the dead to raise up the name of the dead upon his inheritance. (4:3-5)

The kinsman that had a right to redeem and was willing to buy the land answered that he could not continue in the transaction. His explanation was that, in taking Ruth to be his wife, he would jeopardize his own inheritance. It dawned upon this unnamed kinsman that he had two responsibilities, which were joined in one. He had an important role in the property of Elimelech, but also to the widow of one of Elimelech's sons. On his shoulders now rested this two-fold obligation. He could not accept one without the other. Boaz had given the challenge, the kinsman must make the choice of doing the part of a redeemer or not. This was what Boaz intended by mentioning the land first, and later the fact of Ruth being taken as an object of love. Boaz's great love and interest in Ruth shone clearly in his handling of the matter. The kinsman immediately abdicated his rights. To redeem the property he was prepared, but certainly not willing to purchase Ruth the Moabitess. The full act of being the redeemer demanded more than silver, it entailed personal sacrifice, and great love.

It is necessary to consider the qualifications of the "go'el" (redeemer) and the "levir" (a husband's brother). These two important family institutions require careful study, otherwise a clear understanding of the falling short of the nameless kinsman is inexplicable. In the full work of a kinsman-redeemer a search for one to have the requirements gave rise to three questions: 1. Was there a kinsman with the rights? 2. Was there a kinsman with the ability? 3. Was there a kinsman with the willingness?

1. **He must have rights.** It is evident that one might be rich but could not redeem because he was not a kinsman. Boaz was one with these rights as also was the other kinsman and likely others. The right to redeem (ga'el) was unique to the kinsman-redeemer (go'el). These great words are used of our Lord Jesus Christ: *I will help thee, saith the Lord and thy Redeemer (Isaiah 41:14)*. Our glorious Lord became the near Kinsman. *When the fullness of the time was come God sent forth His Son, born of a woman, born under the law, to redeem them which were under the law, that we might receive the adoption of sons (Galatians 4:4,5)*. *For there is one God and one Mediator between God and men, – Himself man, Christ Jesus, who gave Himself a ransom for all (1 Timothy 2:5,6 R.V.)*. Also in the great prophetic Book of Isaiah, where over twenty times we read of the Redeemer, the redeemed or redemption, reference is made to the Kinsman character of the Lord. *Unto us a Child is born, unto us a Son is given (Isaiah 9:6)*. *Behold a virgin shall conceive, and bear a son, and shall call His name Immanuel (Isaiah 7:14)*. Thus God sets forth the rights of His Son to redeem, foreshadowed in Boaz.

2. **He must have ability.** Boaz had the rights. He was a go'el, but without the means, he could never have accomplished redemption. However, early in the book we read of him as *a mighty man of wealth (Ruth 2:1)*. The first mention of him informs the reader of the ample resources of the go'el. He prefigures in his wealth the risen glorified One in Heaven, whose riches are unsearchable (Ephesians 3:8).

3. **He must have willingness.** A kinsman with rights and riches, yet without a willing heart, was unfit to redeem. The other kinsman was unwilling, hence he was forced to pass the position of go'el to Boaz, who was willing to make the sacrifice. His act was one of love, Boaz was the only one with rights, riches and readiness. The Saviour, whose love to the utmost was tried, shines forth in this ancient type. He is the only Redeemer.

We must now consider a problem concerning which various ideas have been suggested. Who does the kinsman who failed to redeem represent? Some describe the nearer kinsman as the law, but the law was unable to redeem whereas the kinsman was able, but unwilling. If, as others have stated, he be a picture of Adam or the natural man, the same principle obviates the application.

And the kinsman said, I cannot redeem it for myself, lest I mar mine own inheritance: redeem thou my right to thyself, for I cannot redeem it. Now this was the manner in former time in Israel concerning redeeming and concerning changing, for to confirm all things: a man plucked off his shoe, and gave it to his neighbor, and thus was a testimony in Israel. Therefore the kinsman said unto Boaz, buy it for thee. So he drew off his shoe. (4:6-8).

The name of the nearer kinsman was doubtless known to Boaz, but the inspired writer was guided to leave him in anonymity. The purpose of the transaction between Boaz and the unnamed kinsman was to bring to light the absolute supremacy of Boaz. He was the only one who was able and willing to redeem. The same idea of exalting the Lamb as the only worthy One, by eliminating all others for whom search may be made, is evident. In the words of Revelation 5:2-6. "Who is worthy?" No one in heaven, nor in earth neither under the earth was able to open the book. Finally, the Lamb in the midst of the throne displays His supremacy and the song of redemption begins. It is our conclusion that the identity of the nearer kinsman as a type of the law is not the objective of the narrative, but rather to extol Boaz as the only redeemer.

The verbal withdrawal of the go'el to redeem was finalized by the ceremony of the shoe. All the people present and the ten elders would be so impressed with this symbolic action of validation that they could ever after testify to a completed transaction.

The removing of the sandal and passing it to Boaz indicated the rights of Boaz to walk on the land as his own. The kinsman had surrendered his claim upon the whole inheritance, even to a foot's breadth. It is interesting to compare the mention of the foot-breadth as the minimum holding of land which a man might possess as an inheritance in the words of God to Moses (Deuteronomy 2:5).

And Boaz said unto the elders, and unto all the people. Ye are witnesses this day, that I have bought all that was Elimelech's, and all that was Chilion's and Mahlon's at the hand of Naomi. Moreover, Ruth the Moabitess, the wife of Mahlon have I purchased to be my wife, to raise up the name of the dead upon his inheritance, that the name of the dead be not cut off from among the brethren, and from the gate of his place: ye are witnesses this day. And all the people that were in the gate, and the elders, said, We are witnesses. The Lord make the woman that is come into thy house like Rachel and like Leah, which two did build the house of Israel; and do thou worthily Ephratah, and be famous in Bethlehem. And let thy house be like the house of Pharez whom Tamar bare unto Judah, of the seed which the Lord shall give thee of this young woman. (4:9-12)

How this beautiful book ends is exquisite and of great value and interest in the divine arrangement of material in most books of the Bible. The beginning and ending have links, and usually the end is better than the beginning, Solomon recognized this principle when he stated, *Better is the end of a thing than the beginning thereof* (*Ecclesiastes* 7:8). The conclusion is validating and joyful, finalized with what seems to most students to be the author's purpose, to provide an account of David's genealogy. Here we have the ultimate, the royal line of Judah through which David would come, and Christ the Messiah Himself.

The first three chapters are dominated by pictures of Ruth as a stranger afar off, an alien brought near, a gleaner in the field of Boaz and a worshipper at the feet of the redeemer. In this closing chapter Boaz is preeminent, the Holy Spirit directs us to his claim (verse 9), his reclaim (verse 11), and his name (verse 14). Boaz is a beautiful figure of our Lord Jesus Christ, who became the Kinsman-Redeemer, and purchased the field (the world) and the pearl (the bride) with His own blood (Matthew 13:44,46).

The scene in the gate was a wonderful witness to the competence of Boaz. The ten elders and all the people who had seen the "ceremony of the shoe," and "the purchase of the land and wife" by Boaz expressed their desire for Jehovah's blessing upon Him and Ruth, and all His house.

The response of the Bethlehemites to the unfolding of redeeming love, was expressed in a delightful benediction and prayer. Although Ruth is a small book, prayer is one of the evidences of remnant testimony in those days when every man did what was right in his own eyes. Surely an example for all time, the Spirit of God would underscore six prayers in the book:

1. **Naomi's Prayer:** *The Lord deal kindly with you...The Lord grant you that ye may find rest (1: 2-9).*

2. **The Reapers' Prayer:** *The Lord bless thee (2:4).*

3. **Boaz's Prayer:** *The Lord recompense thy work, and a full reward be given thee of the Lord God of Israel, under whose wings thou art come to trust (2:12).*

4. **Naomi's Prayer:** *Blessed be he of the Lord, who hath not left off His kindness to the living and to the dead (2:20).*
5. **Boaz's Prayer:** *Blessed be thou of the Lord my daughter (3:10).*
6. **Elder's Prayer:** *The Lord make the woman that is come into thy house like Rachel (4:11,12).*

It can be seen that this spirit of prayer was associated with various aspects of life. Some were offered in seasons of sadness, others in days of joy. They touched daily tasks, social relationships, personal and family living, bereavement and marriage. The Lord Jesus said, *Men ought always to pray and not faint (Luke 18:1).* This is clearly illustrated in the spirit of prayer evident in the Book of Ruth in every chapter.

The threefold desire of the hearts of the townsfolk of Bethlehem for the blessing of God upon the bride and the bridegroom and their future is a benediction suitable for a union in the Lord.

Since marriage was ordained by God, it is becoming that it should always be accompanied with God's blessing and the presence of Christ (John 2:1,2). Yet alas! in these latter times marriage has been degraded to a mere civil contract, or ignored altogether.

The first desire of the assembly in the gate was that the childless young widow might be fruitful as Rachel and Leah, from whose sons came eight tribes of the Nation of Israel. Rachel died in the child-bearing of Benjamin and was buried near Bethlehem (Genesis 35:19). For this cause it would appear that mention of her name is given priority over Leah, who was her elder sister. The prayer of their heart was that Ruth would be fruitful in bearing children, *for children are an heritage of the Lord, and the fruit of the womb is his reward (Psalm 127:3).* It is a sad record of society today that multitudes of lives are legally destroyed in the womb. One hospital may have a staff working to help babies survive, and have another area where babies are murdered. Every Christian must believe in the sanctity of life in the womb. No Christian doctor should ever be implicated in abortion, for life is in the hand of God alone. The people realized the importance of the child's birth in Israel, not only to continue the nation, but because through Israel Messiah would be born.

The second desire of all the people in the gate was that Boaz himself would have power in Ephratah, and would be famous in Bethlehem. The word "famous" literally means "to call a name or make a name to sound." These words are prophetic, for thence came the birth of Him who has made Bethlehem famous in all the world and to all eternity.

Finally, their prayer for the family yet to be expressed great faith. They desired that Boaz whom, it would seem, was childless, would like his ancestor Pharez have numerous descendants. Among the descendants of Pharez, who himself was the second son of Judah, came Boaz (chapter 4:18-21), the type of Christ the Redeemer, and later Jashobeam, "Chief of all the Captains of the Host" (1 Chronicles 11:11). What a beautiful type of Christ as "Chiefest among ten thousand (myriads)" (Song of Solomon 5:10)!

The similarities between the Book of Ruth and the Prophecy of Isaiah have often been mentioned, the subject of both being the Redeemer, Redemption, and the Redeemed.

We would particularly associate the benediction of the witnesses of Boaz, the only saviour of Ruth, with the words of Jehovah in Isaiah, *I am the Lord and beside Me there is no Saviour; and you are my witnesses* (Isaiah 43:11-12). We have stated that Boaz is a delightful type of our Lord Jesus Christ as our Kinsman Redeemer. One way of interpreting Old Testament pictures of the Lord Jesus is by comparison, which is the usual method. However, by contrasting Christ with men of other ages, it is even more interesting and adds to the uniqueness of the Lord.

Boaz had no sufferings to endure, nor death to pass through, to gain his bride. The Lord Jesus endured the cross to obtain His bride. The purchase of redemption by Boaz was no doubt by giving out of his wealth, silver and gold, although the actual price was undisclosed. The Lord Jesus shed His precious blood to redeem. This mighty sum is disclosed in the scripture, and valued by His people (1 Peter 1:18,19; Revelation 5:9). The law stated that a kinsman who failed to redeem and take his brother's wife, to raise up unto his brother a name in Israel, would be subject to shame and spitting before the elders of his city (Deuteronomy 25:5-9). No such open scorn would ever be given to one like Boaz, who was willing to redeem, according to the divine requirements. In view of this, how shameful the treatment given to our blessed Lord, when proud men spit into the face of the glorious Redeemer! How serious and dreadful the sin of the rejection of that Messiah by the representatives of the nation of Israel!

The blessed Redeemer hid not his face from shame and spitting (Isaiah 50:6). He anticipated such treatment, *They shall mock Him, and shall scourge Him and shall spit upon Him (Mark 10:34)*. Twice this indignity was meted to Him. First, by the servants of Israel's High Priest, when some *began to spit on Him, and to cover His face, and to buffet Him, and to say unto Him, Prophesy: and the servants did strike Him with the palms of their hands (Mark 14:65)*. Again, some hours later, in the midst of Roman soldiers, in the courtyard of the palace of Pilate, the whole band smote the Saviour upon His thorn-crowned *head with a reed, and did spit upon Him (Mark 15:19)*.

As we contemplate such boundless love and unequaled shame, we bow our hearts in the presence of this One whose grace far exceeded that of Boaz. The precious words of R.C. Chapman express these scenes of shame:

125

That visage married, those sorrows deep,
The thorns, the scourge, the gall,
These were the golden chains of love
His captive to enthrall.

Fain would I strike the golden harp
And wear the promised crown:
And at Thy feet while bending low,
Would sing what grace has done.

As we contrast the vast gulf between Boaz and Christ in paying the price of redemption, other aspects of the supremacy of the Lord Jesus become evident.

There is a contrast of birth. Of Boaz we read: *Salmon begat Boaz of Rahab (Matthew 1:5)*; whereas of Christ, we read, *And Jacob begat Joseph the husband of Mary, of whom (singular) was born Jesus (Matthew 1:16)*. Boaz was born of usual generation, but his mother had been once a harlot. But our Lord Jesus was born of woman (Galatians 4:4) without an earthly father and His mother was a virgin (Isaiah 7:14, Matthew 1:23).

Boaz was a man of great wealth and affluence, with property, prosperity, and power, but Christ was in the world in poverty, living in obscurity, wearied with His journey, penniless, hungry, thirsty, and having nowhere to lay His head. *Ye know the grace of our Lord Jesus Christ, that, though He was rich, yet for your sakes, he became poor, that ye through His poverty might be rich (2 Corinthians 8:9)*. What a contrast in lifestyle! Boaz never became poor.

II. THE SATISFACTION OF THE REDEEMER

So Boaz took Ruth, and she became his wife... and she bare a son. And the woman said unto Naomi, Blessed be the Lord, which hath

not left thee this day without a kinsman, that his name may be famous in Israel. And he shall be unto thee a restorer of thy life, and a nourisher of thine old age: for thy daughter-in-law, which loveth thee is better to thee than seven sons, hath born him. And Naomi took the child, and laid it in her bosom, and became nurse unto it. And the women her neighbors gave it a name saying, There is a son born to Naomi, and they called his name Obed. He is the father of Jesse, and the father of David. (4:13-17)

In this delightful section the satisfaction of the redeemer and the redeemed is the blessed theme: 1. Boaz found satisfaction in the completion of his purposes in obtaining a bride; 2. Ruth was satisfied with his person; 3. The women of Bethlehem were satisfied with the blessing of God among them.

This precious truth is presented beautifully in Ruth. At the beginning of the book she is a childless widow, now at the end she is a mother with a child. In chapter one, we are called to witness a burial; in chapter four, we are called to witness a birth.

Boaz took Ruth, and she became his wife: and he went in unto her, and the Lord (Jehovah) gave her conception, and she bare a son. (4:13)

Ruth was no longer spoken of as "Ruth the Moabitess," but "Ruth the wife of Boaz." All her enrichment and enjoyment came from her union with the redeemer.

One preeminent theme which dominates the Book of Ruth is the hand of God working behind the scenes. He is the hidden Controller of lives. God's divine providence is given special emphasis in the book. The history compares with that of Joseph, where God worked in an unperceived manner; but finally revealed His purpose (Genesis 45:5). It seems evident that the main object of the narra-

127

tive is brought to light in these closing verses. The result of the union of Ruth and Boaz leads on to the record of the royal line of Judah, through which David would come, and through David would come Christ, the Messiah.

Twice only in the book is direct reference made to the intervention of God in a special way, and both references have to do with barren conditions. The first is the famine condition in the land of Israel, when the Lord visited His people in providing a harvest (chapter 1:6). The words, "The Lord had visited His people" connect with the Gospel of Luke, "God hath visited His people" (Luke 7:16). Such a comparison cannot fail to draw the reader's mind onward from the history of Boaz and Ruth to that of Christ.

The final record of Jehovah's superintending grace is the bringing of Ruth from barrenness to fruitfulness, by His enablement. "The Lord gave her conception and she bare a son." Again the reader's thoughts are projected forward to the more miraculous birth of the Son of God, who entered into humanity by means of the virgin birth. Obed was begotten by Boaz of Ruth, but the Saviour was born of a woman without an earthly father. *When the fullness of the time was come, God sent forth His Son, born of a woman* (Galatians 4:4).

The wonderful, prayerful benediction of the women of Bethlehem is in contrast to their first greeting, *Is this Naomi?* (1:19), as they looked upon her appearance, changed through sorrow and bitterness, she whose name means "pleasant." These same matrons of Bethlehem now join in congratulating her. Naomi becomes the focus of attention, while Ruth's name is not mentioned in their blessing. In this section of the book, Naomi's name is thrice recorded. The many blessings bestowed through Jehovah's grace are forthcoming in the son born. To Naomi he was to be a true kinsman. The women requested of the Lord that his name would be famous in Israel. This fame was required, for he became a progenitor of David's

Son and David's Lord.

Naomi would find in him restoration of life and nourishment in old age. Renewal and security was promised. Jehovah, whom she had blamed for dealing bitterly, had finally dealt bountifully.

These women were not chattering gossips of the town, but godly souls with an understanding of God's purposes in this exceptional birth of Abraham's seed of promise. No finer tribute could have been paid to Ruth than their words to Naomi, "Thy daughter-in-law, which loveth thee, which is better to thee than seven sons hath born him." Coming from these women of Bethlehem, who at the first must have envied Ruth and seen in her union with the man of wealth a slight upon their own daughters, it has a splendid testimony to the qualities of mind and manner possessed by Ruth.

Then Naomi took the child, and laid it in her bosom, and became nurse unto it. (4:16)

Naomi's maternal feelings were aroused towards Ruth's child. All her interests were in the babe. Her warm-hearted reflection gave her a readiness to devote her time and effort to nursing the child for the Lord. She became to Obed what Lois became centuries later to Timothy (2 Timothy 1:5).

Among young believers, spiritual nursing is one of the greatest needs of these evil days of moral decline and departure, as in the days of Obed. Moses used the idea of leadership as nursing in the wilderness, the thousands of Israel: *Carrying them in My bosom, as a nursing father beareth the sucking child unto the land (Numbers 11:12).* Concerning the glorious work of Christ we read: *He shall gather the lambs with His arm, and carry them in His bosom (Isaiah 40:11).* Paul described his early ministry to the new believers at Thessalonica as the care of a nursing mother with her own children (1 Thessalonians 2:7).

Miriam saw the need of a nurse for her brother, when he wept, on the occasion of the discovery by Pharaoh's daughter of the babe in the ark of bulrushes among the flags of the Nile. The commission of the princess to the mother of the child was, *Take this child away and nurse it for me (Exodus 2:6-10)*. The nursing of Jochebed proved effectual in the preparation of Moses for his life's work for God. The important responsibility of nursing young believers, and feeding them with the milk of the Word, requires special mention in the churches of God. The example of Naomi indicates affection, as she took the child and laid him in her bosom, as her own. This warm-hearted attitude towards the young among the saints produces mutual understanding and fellowship. It has been said, "There is no better way to get a new lease on life than to start investing yourself in the younger generation."

Naomi was no longer Mara, and Ruth rejoiced at God's special gift, her son. The sure and bountiful reward was given by the Lord God of Israel as predicted by Boaz (chapter 2:12). Who ever came under His wings in vain? Who ever lost by trusting Him? Who ever forsook the world for the Kingdom of God, and did not rejoice in the exchange?

The women of Bethlehem selected a name for the child, which was acceptable to Naomi, Boaz and Ruth, unlike the name chosen by the neighbors of Elizabeth in later days for her child — a name rejected by the parents because of the Lord's instruction (Luke 1:59,60). This name, Obed, was acceptable to God, a name meaning worshipper and servant. These two features sum up godly living. This combination was referred to by the Lord Jesus; when tempted by Satan, He quoted from the scriptures, *It is written, thou shalt worship the Lord thy God, and Him only shalt thou serve* (Deuteronomy 6:13, Matthew 4:10). Obed was the father of Jesse, and Jesse would have eight sons, the youngest of whom would be David, the shepherd king (1 Samuel 16:6-13). Of David, as concerning the flesh, came Jesus the Christ, the Light of the Gentiles and the glory of Israel, Who is over all, God blessed forever (Romans 1:3, Romans 9:5).

There is one other lesson to be learned by the birth of Obed. Every time we look upon a newborn child, we realize God has a plan for that child. Who can foresee the potential of a newborn soul? What will the final outcome be in testimony, missionary enterprise or evangelism? Never underestimate the power and purposes of the Lord. Before leaving this section, a survey of the book presents Boaz the bridegroom in some distinct pen pictures foreshadowing the presentation of our Lord Jesus Christ in the Gospels and the Epistles of Paul:

1. The mighty man of wealth (Ruth 2:1) — Christ in Matthew (Matthew 28);

2. The man of activity (Ruth 3:18) — Christ in Mark (Mark 1:3);

3. The man, the Kinsman (Ruth 2:20) — Christ in Luke (Luke 1:3);

4. The lover of his bride (Ruth 4:10) — Christ in John (John 13:1);

5. The man of unlimited redemption (Romans);

6. The man of unifying Lordship (Corinthians);

7. The man of undisputed relationship (Galatians);

8. The man of unsearchable riches (Ephesians);

9. The man of unassuming service (Philippians);

10. The man of unequalled preeminence (Colossians);

11. The man of undivided affection (Thessalonians).

Ruth, as his bride, foreshadows the beautiful truth of the church as the bride of Christ, and links her to six other brides who form a lengthy picture of the glorious call and destiny of the believers of the present age:

1. Eve - The Formation of the Church (Genesis 2:21-23,

Ephesians 5:31);

2. Rachel - The Favour of the Church (Genesis 29:20, Ephesians 5:25);

3. Rebekah - The Faith of the Church (Genesis 24:53, 1 Peter 1:8);

4. Asenath - The Fruit of the Church (Genesis 41:50, Colossians 1:6);

5. Zipporah - The fidelity of the Church (Exodus 2:21,22, Ephesians 5:25);

6. Ruth - The Future of the Church (Ruth 4:9,10; Revelation 19:7);

7. Pharaoh's Daughter - The final Destiny of the Church (1 Kings 7:8; John 14:1).

III. THE SELECTION OF THE REDEMPTIVE LINE

Now these are the generations of Pharez: Pharez begat Nezron and Hezron begat Ram and Ram begat Amminadab and Amminadab begat Nahshon, and Nahshon begat Salmon, and Salmon begat Boaz, and Boaz, and Boaz begat Jesse, and Jesse begat David. (4:18-22)

The Book of Ruth ends with a short genealogy. Genealogies are often passed over as unimportant and uninteresting. Agur's inspired testimony clarifies the value of every word of God, *Every word of God is pure (Proverbs 30:5)*. With this also Paul's testimony to his spiritual son, Timothy, agrees, *All scripture is given by inspiration of God, and is profitable for doctrine, for reproof, for correction, for instruction in righteousness (2 Timothy 3:16)*. There is therefore nothing in the scriptures which does not have a good purpose. That which may seem unprofitable, if considered diligently will render useful teaching. This is true of the subject of scripural chronology. This genealogy at the close of the Book of Ruth is exactly repeated in Matthew 1:4-6.

The phrase "These are the generations of" or similar phrases occur often in the Old Testament. First: *These are the generations of the heavens and the earth (Genesis 2:4)*, followed by ten other occasions which present the tenfold division of the remainder of Genesis. One of the most important is described as "The Book of the generations of Adam." This has been described as the Book of Death (Romans 5:12).

The New Testament opens with a similar formula to Genesis 5:1; "The Book of the Generations of Jesus Christ" (Matthew 1:1). This could be rightly called "The Book of Life." Genealogies indicate the idea of developing history leading to a final event of vital importance. The Holy Spirit often omitted many names and even generations. This is true in this genealogy in Ruth.

The lesson taught is that genealogies are often representative; every detail is not given, but what is given is of spiritual value, especially emphasizing the scarlet thread of redemption and the purple line of royalty.

It is interesting to consider the list of these ten generations — they may be divided into two groups of six and four. The first six names, from Pharez to Salmon, are linked with Egypt and the wilderness. The second list of four names, from Boaz to David, cover a period of over 300 years. The historical reference to the names listed is informative and important: "Pharez begat Hezron" (verse 18). Pharez's birth shows him to be the son of Judah and Tamar, and twin brother of Zerah, over whom he was given precedence (Genesis 38:29). Pharez, and not his father, Judah, heads this genealogy. Judah died before the Exodus, and before Israel as a nation began. Hezron was Pharez's first born son and he begat Ram of Aram (Matthew 1:3). Amminadab's daughter was Aaron's wife (Exodus 6:23). Amminadab begat Naashon (verse 20). This man became prince of the tribe of Judah in the wilderness (Numbers 1:7, 1 Chronicles 2:10). Salmon has been mentioned by Jewish historians as being one of the two spies who lodged in Rahab's house (Joshua 2:1). He married Rahab, the former harlot. Boaz was the son of Rahab and Salmon. Boaz begat Obed of Ruth, and Obed begat Jesse who had eight sons, the youngest being David, who became king over all Israel. He was chosen by God to be the shepherd ruler of His people. *He chose David also his servant, and took him from the sheepfolds: From following the ewes great with young, he brought him to feed Jacob his people, and Israel his inheritance. So he fed them according to the integrity of his heart, and guided them by the skillfulness of his hands* (Psalm 78:70-72).

David had the knowledge that the Messiah would be of the tribe of Judah (Genesis 49:10). *Judah prevailed above his brethren and of him came the chief ruler* (1 Chronicles 5:2). No one in Israel knew the exact family of Judah through which Messiah would come until it was revealed to David (2 Samuel 7:12-17). Christ is called the Son of David (Matthew 15:22) and will finally sit upon the throne of David as King of Kings and the Lion of the tribe of Judah (Revelation 5:4-6).

The intention therefore of this genealogy is to confirm the truth of Jacob's prophecy of Shiloh. The Man of Peace, the Messiah, will come from the royal tribe of Judah. Hence it commences with Pharez, the son of Judah, and ends with David, whose Son was to be the Messiah, as is believed by all who accept the veracity of scripture.

There seems a difficulty in the minds of many students to see how four generations could cover the long period between Rahab and David. How can this genealogy be reconciled with chronology? Two answers have been offered:

1. Some have stated that Boaz was not the son of Rahab, but her great-grandson. Their suggestion is that Rahab was Boaz's "mother"

134

in the sense that she was his ancestress. The expression "our father Abraham" is used to enforce this idea (Romans 4:12).

2. Others have affirmed that each of the four persons mentioned from the coming of Israel into Canaan until the birth of David, must have begotten children when upwards of 100 years old. It may have been an act of God to grant children in old age to these godly ancestors of Christ, for whose birth His people waited patiently for hundreds of years.

Abraham had many children from Keturah after Sarah's death when he was well over 100 years of age (Genesis 25:1-7). It seems credible that in those days of longevity, men had children at such an age. Which of these two opinions is preferable we leave to the judgment of the student reader.

The names of four women are mentioned in the genealogy in Matthew 1, and these four are alluded to in chapter 4 of Ruth: Tamar (Ruth 4:12) was the mother of Pharez (Matthew 1:3); Salmon (Ruth 4:21) was the husband of Rahab (Matthew 1:5); Boaz (Ruth 4:21) was the husband of Ruth (Matthew 1:5); David (Ruth 4:22) was the husband of Bathsheba (Matthew 1:6).

Women's names were never written in Jewish genealogies, but here their inclusion tells the wondrous story of grace, and the union of both Jew and Gentile in Christ. Tamar, Rahab, and the former wife of Urias, were sinful women. Ruth was nationally an alien idolater. Rahab was a Canaanite and Ruth a Moabitess, both were Gentiles. What wondrous grace that they who once were morally unfit were saved and linked with Christ! This same grace which brought these outcast women into divine relationship with our Lord Jesus Christ is available to every type of sinner in every place who will trust Him as Saviour and Lord.

The last word in the delightful book of Ruth is "David." The misrule of the age of no king as outlined in Judges (Judges 21:25) was brought to an end when God's King appears as seen in David, but before that could take place, Saul, man's choice of king, would be enthroned.

Our day is marked by the rejection of the King, which has led to an abounding of lawlessness. Soon the world will accept the false king. Days of increasing violence will result. God's King will finally appear to judge the world and to reign from shore to shore as the Prince of Peace.

This Book of Ruth teaches that, while we are presently living in an evil age, comparable with the days of the judges, when there was no king in Israel, and every man doing what was right in his own eyes, we can be as the godly Naomi, Ruth and Boaz — devoted subjects of the absent King and serving His kingdom.

The first chapter describes the death of Elimelech, whose name means "My God is the King." But in this last chapter, the book ends with the birth of David, whose name means "beloved" and who is God's glorious type of the King of kings and Lord of lords.

As with gladness men of old
Did the guiding star behold,
As with joy they hailed its light
Leading onward, beaming bright
So, most gracious Lord may we
Evermore be led to Thee.

Study Chart

	Chapter 1	Chapter 2	Chapter 3	Chapter 4
Historical	Ruth's Resolve	Ruth's Resources	Ruth's Request	Ruth's Reward
Personal	Her Widowhood	Her Works	Her Worth	Her Worthiness
Inheritance	Left Behind	Lost a While	Longed After	Love's Purchase
Redemption	Required	Revealed	Reserved	Realized
Lessons	God Chosen	Gleaning in the Word of God	Grace claiming redemptive priviledges	Glory Shared
Application	Life's Supreme confession is to acknowledge the Lordship of Christ.	Gleaning in the Scriptures for sustenance, brings into the presence of the Lord of the Harvest	Approaching the Redeemer requires preparation, reverence and faith	The final aspect of redemption will be enjoyed when the Redeemer receives the bride unto Himself. Later His name will be famous in Israel.

Bibliography

Anderson, R. *Ruth.* USA: Baker Bookhouse, 1970.

Atkinson, David. *Wings of Refuge.* England: Inter-Varsity Press, 1983.

Coates, C. A. *Outline of Ruth.* London: Moorish Press, 1929.

David, John D. *Dictionary of the Bible.* Westminster Press, 1940.

Henry, Matthew. *Commentary.* New York: Revell Publishing

Hocking, W. J. *Book of Ruth.* England: Mayflower Press, 1947.

Mathieson, Alfred. *Romance of Redemption.* Pickering and Inglis, 1915.

Moorehouse, Henry. *Ruth the Moabitess.* London: Morgan and Scott, 1900.

Mauro, Philip. *Ruth.* Boston: Hamilton Press, 1920.

Morgan, Campbell. *Analyzed Bible.* fleming Revell, 1964.

Petrie, Arthur. *Ruth Redeemed.* Seattle, WA 1867.

Rideout, Samuel. *Ruth.* USA: Bible Truth Publishers, 1900.

Ritchie, John. *Ruth.* Kilmarnock: John Ritchie, 1910.

Van Ryn, August. *Boaz and Ruth.* New York: Loizeaux, 1950.

Scripture Index

Subject Index